Para
Esteban Escamilla

Pa'lante Siempre —
"Escribe lo que
siente —"

Con Respeto
Un Hermano Mas

Piri Thomas

Stories from El Barrio

Other books by Piri Thomas

■

Down These Mean Streets
Savior, Savior, Hold My Hand
Seven Long Times

STORIES FROM EL BARRIO

by Piri Thomas

ALFRED A. KNOPF
NEW YORK

To my darling wife, Suzie Dod Thomas,
for all your creative help in the "refination" of
Stories from El Barrio

This is a Borzoi Book published by Alfred A. Knopf, Inc.

 Published in the United States by Alfred A. Knopf, Inc., New York, and simultaneously in Canada by Random House of Canada Limited, Toronto. Distributed by Random House, Inc., New York. Manufactured in the United States of America

Library of Congress Cataloging in Publication Data
Thomas, Piri, 1928– Stories from El Barrio. Contents: The three mosquiteers.—The konk.—Putting it on for Juanita.—Amigo brothers. [etc.] 1. Spanish Americans in New York (City)—Juvenile fiction. [1. Spanish Americans in New York (City)—Fiction. 2. Short stories] I. Title. PZ7.T3693St [Fic] 78-3287
ISBN 0-394-83568-9
3 5 7 9 10 8 6 4 2

Introduction

The stories in this book have to do with the fantasies and illusions, as well as the harsh realities that were so much a part of my life growing up in the barrios of *Nueva Yawk* 50 years ago. While the drugs of choice and some of the language may have changed, conditions in the ghetto today remain pretty much the same as then: poverty, racism, violence. In fact, some things may have gotten worse.

The reader will find that *Stories from El Barrio* accurately represents the conflicts and aspirations faced by young people today and, I hope, offers insight into the common humanity of us all.

So I say to the children of all ages and color:

Doubt not your creative beauty and allow no one to doubt for you. For if you are what you eat you also are what you think. So, por favor, don't mug your minds.

Your bro,
PIRI THOMAS

Contents

CONTENTS

Stories from El Barrio

■ I ■
The Three Mosquiteers

Pedro moved about the small apartment like a shadow, careful not to wake his family. He showered quickly and then ate a breakfast of wheat flakes, followed by a cup of cocoa and two slices of hot buttered toast, thick with sweet grape jam. He could have eaten more, but his stomach was so excited he didn't have his usual appetite.

Today was the Great March, his first adventure as a new-born tenderfoot. He proudly recalled the candlelit Indian ceremony, when he and his best friend Johnny Cruz were inducted into Troop 633, Wolf Patrol, with the rank of tenderfoot in the Boy Scouts of America.

Pedro glanced at his new boy scout wrist watch. It was 5:30 A.M. He was right on schedule. In his bedroom, which he shared with his younger brother Frankie, he carefully eased a large cardboard box out from under their bed. Proudly, he gave himself ten merits for not having awakened Frankie until he heard his brother's sleepy voice grumbling, "How's a guy supposed to get any sleep with an elephant crashing about?"

Pedro painfully subtracted ten merits from himself, which put him ten merits under a tenderfoot zero.

A rapid knock interrupted his thoughts, and he stumbled toward the front door balancing the large cardboard box in his arms.

"Who is it?" he whispered.

"Cripes sake, *hombre*. Who the hell's it gonna be coming at this time? It's me, Johnny."

"What's the secret password?" Pedro felt like horsing around.

"Your mother," came the ultimate barrio insult.

Pedro opened the door quickly. Johnny gave a friendly three-finger salute in order to avoid any retaliation for his blasphemous choice of a secret password.

"Hey, turkey," Pedro hissed. "Don'tcha know it's too early to be playing games. Don't forget you got a momma too."

Johnny's three-finger salute turned to just his middle finger pointing straight up in the air. He grinned warmly. "Ah, forget it, man. Only playing around. Jesus, ain't you got no sense of humor? Say, what you doing walking around looking like some hairless gorilla?"

Johnny's eyes ran over Pedro's body, draped with a towel. He yanked the towel away leaving Pedro strictly bare-assed.

"*Coño,* Johnny. You sure got up sharp as a tack."

Pedro dropped his cardboard box while grabbing for his covering and began to curse.

"That's a no-no, bro." Johnny gave him the boy scout sign with both hands held high. "Profanity is not for us. Tenderfoots are gentlemen who help old ladies across the street instead of mugging them."

"Yeah, yeah. And tenderfeet don't hurt other people's feelings by putting down their mothers."

Johnny changed the subject with surprising ease.

"Hey, you ain't said nothing on how I look."

Pedro had to admit that Johnny looked almost as good as he would if he ever got dressed. Ten minutes later he stood outfitted in his official boy scout uniform complete with knapsack, hatchet, hunting knife, canteen, flashlight, and whistle, all of which had come out of the large, now empty cardboard box. They stood admiring each other while each secretly thought he looked better than the other.

"I dig the short pants. But these woolen socks are something else. Man, are they itchy."

"Why don't you do like I did?" Johnny peeled down his long woolen scout socks to reveal a pair of his mother's nylon stockings underneath. "It keeps your legs from scratching." He grinned.

"That's *mucho* intelligent." Pedro praised him. "You get ten merits."

"My moms suggested it," Johnny admitted honestly.

"You still get ten merits for honesty," Pedro answered quickly.

"Ready to go, bro?" Johnny asked, looking at himself in the small hall mirror.

"Yeah, I'm ready," said Pedro, prancing cool before the same mirror. "Hey, hold it, Johnny.

I forgot to fill my canteen. Er—what's in yours?"

"Ice cold lemonade with mint tea and a haffa pound of *azúcar*. I like it sweet."

Pedro opened the refrigerator hoping to find something that would outdo Johnny's canteen. Triumphantly, he took out a gallon jug of a light brown liquid that had a beerlike foam. It was *maví*, made from an old Puerto Rican recipe of brown sugar, roots, and herbs, boiled and then allowed to ferment. When chilled, it was most refreshing with little bubbles in it—nature's soda pop.

Pedro filled his canteen slowly, careful not to spill any of the *maví*. Johnny watched impatiently and finally said, "Hey, man, it's a quarter to six. Let's shake a leg."

"Coming, man, coming."

Pedro eased his canteen over his head and adjusted his knapsack, into which he had packed quite a few comic books. Looking once more at his reflection, he tilted his ranger hat, smoothed his blue bandana, and felt without a doubt that he was born to be a woodsman He wished his family were awake to check him out. What was the use of looking so great if your folks didn't share in it?

As if his hatchet was reading his thoughts, it

slipped out of its case. It fell noisily to the wooden floor bouncing into a small table. A wine bottle serving as a flower vase toppled and crashed on the floor.

Pedro, holding his breath, listened intently to hear if anyone had awakened. But all to be heard were sounds of sleeping punctuated by heavy snores. Johnny slowly opened the front door and held it for Pedro, who slammed it with a bang. Then, laughing, they both leaped down the stairs, three at a time, and banging against the doors of the other apartments, they clattered through the long dark hallway and out into the early morning sunlight.

They were halfway down the block heading toward the 103rd Street subway station when they heard a roar coming from Pedro's building. They turned. On the fire escape, Pedro's folks, in various stages of dress, were cheering, waving, and smiling, while Frankie was whistling his brains out.

Pedro's face lit up with pleasure. He waved back happily. However the jeers and catcalls from the neighbors awakened by the noise soon dampened his enthusiasm. His heroic vision of triumphantly marching out of the block quickly vanished.

"Shit," he mumbled. "Somebody's gonna get my official boy scout hatchet sunk into their *cabeza*."

Johnny nodded grimly. His right hand curled menacingly around his Jim Bowie scalping knife. They marched to the corner of Lexington Avenue to the tune of whistles, catcalls, and Bronx cheers. Then they stopped.

It was humiliating. Unable to contain themselves, they made an about-face and stood. Pedro pulled out his boy scout whistle and blew on it for all it was worth. Johnny's voice boomed with military precision.

"Atten-shun!" Both tenderfoots snapped to rigid position and saluted smartly.

"About-face. March." Pedro carried on.

The street was suddenly quiet with awed respect. Then it exploded with unanimous cheering. The two scouts did an about-face right out of a West Point ghetto and smartly marched around the corner and disappeared from view. Pedro and Johnny smiled at each other with *mucho gusto*.

As they descended into the dinginess of the 103rd Street station, they shared the same thought.

"Whatcha think, Johnny?" Pedro asked first. "Shall we pull a *bomba*?"

"Let's try it the honest way first," Johnny counseled wisely.

"*Porqué no.*" Pedro smiled, still flushed from the excitement of the triumphant march out of the block.

They approached the subway booth where a man inside his cage was waiting to make change. Johnny saluted with precision.

"We're Boy Scouts, sir," he said.

"I can see that," replied the boothman, unimpressed.

"We're on official business. Troop 633, Wolf Patrol," Pedro added seriously.

"So, good luck," said the man, returning their salute with an ease that bespoke of his familiarity with boy scout traditions.

Both youngsters smiled, pleased at the man's warm sense of comradeship. They walked over to the gate controlled by an electric switch and tugged at it. It refused to open. Pedro looked back and saluted again.

"Ain'tcha gonna open up?" he asked pleasantly.

"What for? You got special passes?"

"Don't need any, do we? We're Boy Scouts on official business." Pedro replied in a voice fast losing faith in the boothman's spirit of brotherhood.

"That and a token will get you guys a ride on this subway line." The boothman laughed while his fingers counted out change.

"Hey, we're only going one stop. You can at least donate that to the Boy Scouts."

"Rules is rules. Just like you got in the Boy Scouts."

"Damn, Sam. You act like the subway company belongs to you." Pedro was getting upset.

"It ain't gonna work. This guy is an ass-kisser for the company," Johnny whispered. "Let's stall till the train comes in."

Pedro nodded. They went through the motion of searching their pockets for change until the soles of their shoes picked up the rumblings of an approaching train. Under the watchful eye of the company man, they made as if to deposit invisible coins in the turnstile. Satisfied, the man glanced away, giving them just enough time to sneak under the barrier while manually turning the turnstile backward over their heads. The sound was enough to make the company man think they had dutifully paid their way.

As they ran for the train, they missed the knowing smile on the boothman's face. He had seen all they had put down, right up to his old trick of turning back the turnstile.

■

The sidewalks around the 92nd Street YMHA were teeming with Boy Scouts from all parts of the city in all sizes, shapes, and colors. Outstanding were the old-timers, resplendent with row upon row of neatly pinned merit badges gleaming on wide sashes that ran from their shoulders across their chests and down to their waists. Each merit was for a different accomplishment: starting fires without matches, swimming, first-aid, cooking, merit badges for everything. The only ones without merits were the shining green tenderfeet who milled around impatiently waiting for the Great March to start so they, too, could begin piling up badges.

Here and there, a shrilling of whistles and barked commands were heard as troop leaders began assembling their columns.

"Okay, okay. Regulars to the front. Tenderfeet to the rear. Line up at ease."

Pedro and Johnny joined forces by mistake with the regulars, the toughened veterans, the *mucho* elite.

"All tenderfeet to the back." A troop leader's sharp eyes escorted the two to their proper place.

Soon there were two divisions the length of the block, regulars in front, tenderfeet closing in the rear. Each platoon was commanded by a troop leader, some hardly older than Pedro, others older than the boothman on 103rd Street.

There was a bit of confusion as scouts attempted to obey simultaneous orders of "Attention" and "At Ease." Finally, the Great Leader Over All, *El Supremo,* emerged with a megaphone in his hand. He was loaded down with merit badges.

"ALL RIGHT, MEN. ATTENSHUN!"

Everybody snapped. Satisfied, the Great Leader, old enough to be a general, creaked out another order.

"ALL RIGHT, MEN. AT EASE. NO TALKING IN LINE."

Pedro hoped *El Supremo* would make up his mind. The knapsack loaded down with comic books was bringing hot-sun sweat to his brow. But he willed it to be as light as air.

The leader continued to blare joyfully into the megaphone. "Members of a time-honored organization, fellow Boy Scouts of America, flowers of American youth. It is with great pleasure that I welcome you on this early Saturday morning. We are about to share an adventure which I . . . er . . . we have named the Great March. Men, set your watches. The Great March starts at 0800 . . ."

"That's 8 A.M.," volunteered Abraham Romero, a tenderfoot.

"No talking in the ranks," barked James Allen, Jr., their troop leader, in a newly acquired position of command.

El Supremo continued. ". . . and from this point on our maps, we will proceed on foot."

"Maps, maps. We ain't got no maps." Pedro panicked. "You got a map, Johnny?"

"No, man. Even if I did, I wouldn't know how to read one."

"We will proceed to the West Side subway, which will take us to the George Washington Bridge. From there we will begin the Great March across into New Jersey and from there to our camp a short skip and a hop away. Are you ready?"

The response was deafening.

"All right. Ready, men. Get set, march. Hup, two, three, four . . ."

The leader began a croaking marching song which was followed, out of tune, by a multitude of voices.

Tramp, tramp, tramp, the boys are marching,
Marching along.
Tramp, tramp, tramp, the boys are marching,
Singing our song.
Hup, hup, hup, hup.

By the time they reached the subway station, Pedro's comic books had increased in weight. Bravely, he tried mind over matter since the honor of El Barrio was at stake.

The train unloaded its passengers at the George Washington Bridge. Wherever one looked, there were all kinds of scouts—scouts with long pants, scouts with short pants, even den scouts in blue uniforms with mothers and fathers tagging along.

"Where's the girl scouts?" Pedro asked.

"They got their own camp," replied a sad Wolf Patroller.

"Man, will you look at that bridge. It must be ten miles!" Johnny exclaimed.

Just looking at the length of the bridge made Pedro thirsty. Sweating under the weight of his knapsack, he took the last long swig of *maví* from his canteen, which he had almost emptied on the way to the West Side subway. Deciding it was time to ease off the burden, he quickly hit on the idea of a comic book sale. At the top of his voice, he began to reel off a most heavy sales pitch.

"Getcha red-hot comic books . . . Superman . . . Batman . . . Mutt and Jeff . . . comics for sale cheap. Five cents each or four for a quarter."

The comics vanished like hot cakes, all twenty-one of them. The money was mentally converted into delicious hot dogs brimming with mustard and spicy onions on top of succulent sauerkraut, plus a full canteen of root beer.

El Supremo's megaphone broke in.

"Troop leaders. Line your men up. Double time. Hup-hup."

He paused for effect and then boomed out, "Men, are we or are we not going to cross the bridge with a Boy Scout's song on our lips?"

Cries of "Yeah" resounded. Somebody howled, imitating a wolf, and like a flash, hundreds of scouts jumped into the act. The Great Leader smiled weakly as he courageously kept on singing "Tramp, tramp, tramp." The crowd kept on howling until the whistle blew over the megaphone, signaling the beginning of the Great March.

Halfway across the bridge, Pedro felt like a prisoner of war on a death march. Noting that his friend Johnny was not caving in, he bolstered his own spirits, yelling out loud, "Come on, you bunch of slowpokes. Get the lead out of your behinds."

All he got in reply were some unkind looks and a reprimand from his troop leader, Jimmy Allen, Jr.

"What's the matter, tenderfoot? You bucking for troop leader?"

Jimmy eyed Pedro suspiciously and shouted even louder, "Come on, come on. Move it along."

By the time Troop 633, Wolf Patrol, had reached the Jersey side, it was a bunch of tired tenderfeet, straining to find some shade to collapse under.

In contrast, the leader was cool and collected. A growing rumor was spreading like firewater throughout the ranks that he carried something in his canteen that was very high-proof.

"We're almost there, men." Troop leader Allen kept promising the promised land.

Many miles later, they were knee-deep in a wilderness of bramble bushes in partnership with a forest of trees. Wearily, they let their knapsacks slide from their backs and collapsed beside them. It was a short-lived rest.

"Men, we got our work cut out. First, we clear a place for ourselves and pitch our tents. Then we will dig latrines, collect fire wood, and fetch water."

"Cripes," said Pedro. "I thought there would be toilets."

He made a face of distaste.

"After that, we will start fires for our meal."

El Supremo pointed to several cartons labeled "Pork and Beans," "Franks and Beans," "Beans and Molasses," "Chili and Beans." At their side was a small mountain of frankfurters and rolls. Empty stomachs growled in unison.

The leader continued.

"No matches are to be used in starting fires. It is to be done as prescribed in your boy scout manual by rubbing wood together. Remember, no matches, no cigarette lighters, no magnifying glasses."

Pedro and Johnny looked at each other and thought of many other places they would rather be.

"Aw, it ain't so hard." Abraham smiled at them. "It's been done a lot of times. You get a little dry moss, some wood shavings, a flat board, and a round piece of wood. You make a small round hole in the flat board and stuff in moss and chips or shavings of dry wood. With a pointed piece of twig between the palms of your hands, rolled back and forth, you press the pointed end into the hole. In no time, this causes friction and the moss catches the heat and smolders into embers. The shavings catch fire. You add more shavings, then little twigs, and the fire will grow bigger and bigger until you can put it under the logs. It's really easy."

"Christ sakes. All that sweating for a can of beans," blurted Johnny.

"Franks, too," added Pedro, who had been admiring Abraham's brains.

"*Oye, amigo,*" he whispered, "Are you Jewish kids always this smart?"

Abraham smiled. "Well, I'm Italian and Jewish. Anyway, we learned this survival technique from the Indians."

Half an hour later, the tenderfoots were still rolling the round twigs, but the only heat around was from the burning blisters on searing palms. Pedro struck first and won envious cheers from the others. He fully began to understand why, in days of old, fire was considered sacred. Without matches, it had to be a miracle.

After everyone was overstuffed on franks and beans, *El Supremo* began laying out the day's activities. There were merit badges to be earned in innumerable categories: starting a fire, weaving a basket, tracking a lost group, hiking, first-aid, mountain climbing. Name the merit, for each there was a task.

"Those of you interested in any of the aforementioned, see the troop leader in charge."

"What are you going out for, Pedro?" Johnny asked.

"I think I'm going out for getting tracked. Let them find me."

"I'm with you." Johnny slapped skin with his partner and with Abraham who decided to join them. Troop Leader Jimmy Allen, Jr., and five other tenderfeet agreed to track them down.

Trooper Jimmy instructed them. "Check your compasses. Wherever you go, follow your compass needle southeast and you can't miss—I hope. If you do get lost, make a small fire and send up smoke signals."

"We ain't got no matches," ventured Johnny.

"Don't worry," Abraham reassured them, his voice dropping to a whisper. "I got a magnifying glass." He tapped his thick eye glasses.

"Okay, fellows. You got a half hour start. Leave some kind of trail. Break twigs, nothing too obvious. Make it hard for us to track you, but not impossible. Got it?"

Jimmy pointed a long finger toward the wilderness.

All three nodded and with compasses, knives, and hatchets bumping lumps all over their bodies, they took off like Buck Rogers.

"Let's turn it around on them," Pedro suggested, as they jogged into the forest. "Like in the movies. We'll back track, set up false trails, maybe even set up a couple of Malaysian tiger traps for them."

"What kind of traps?" asked a worried Abraham. "I really don't want this to get out of hand and become serious enough to constitute any real danger to anyone."

"Okay, no traps." Johnny agreed reluctantly. Like Pedro, he had been visualizing cleverly covered grass pits with sharpened stakes lining the bottom, or even a sling trap set off by tripping a rope that would send a barrage of poisoned arrows toward the trackers.

"How about walking backwards? One guy carries the other two and each takes turns. We'll drive them crazy wondering where the other two went," suggested Pedro.

"That ain't too bad," Johnny agreed. "Or we could dig shallow graves and bury ourselves. Let them pass us and we come in from behind for the massacre."

Now that the game was not going to involve needless mutilations, Abraham was caught up in the spirit.

"Wish we had some ground red pepper for the dogs they'll use to hunt us down."

Soon the conversation faltered, so Pedro seized the initiative. "Come on, fellers, let's move it. We've got lots of territory to cover before our half hour is up. We're supposed to leave signs, ain't we?"

Pedro picked up a piece of rock and scratched in the dirt, "Pedro was here. T. 633."

"Hey *amigos,*" said Abraham. "Let's one of us climb a tree and see just how far behind they are."

Pedro made a three-ring sign with his fingers and immediately volunteered for the dangerous assignment, his eye on a merit badge for guts.

"Naw, let me do it," said Johnny.

"Well, it was my idea," countered Abraham.

"But I volunteered first," Pedro declared stubbornly.

For a tense moment, the three tenderfoot buddies glared at each other in an eye-ball showdown that made the famous shoot-out at the O.K. Corral look like a game of jumping jacks.

Abraham's brains saved the day. "What are we arguing about? With all the trees around, let's each of us pick a tree. After all, three can see much better than just one."

"Yeah, let's climb us each a tree and see what

we can see. Grab a tree for each of you and I'll grab a tree for me."

"Damn, Johnny, you're a poet," Pedro grinned.

"Not bad, not bad," praised Abraham, mumbling something in Italian under his breath.

"*Muchas gracias, amigos.*" Johnny bowed and made a mighty leap toward a branch, psyching himself into being Tarzan or one of his apes. Unfortunately, the heavy branch was a dead one, and the cracking of dry wood and the crashing to the ground of Johnny were as one.

"You okay?" Abraham was genuinely alarmed, while Pedro fought hard to keep a straight face. Johnny quickly picked himself up from the ground. He was not hurt, only his cool took a beating.

He leaped again, but this time he chose a branch sturdy enough to hold a flying horse. The other two climbed their tree without mishap.

"Do you see anything?" asked Pedro.

"I can make out the scout flag at the camp," shouted Abraham. "Wait, I can see them now. They are in a ravine."

"Yeah, yeah, but more like a trench," shouted Johnny from his tree.

"Well, let's get out of here," Pedro said, trembling with excitement.

It was a real chase now, something like the Seventh Cavalry versus the Apaches.

"Remember, we got to leave some kind of trail, nothing too obvious."

No sooner were the words out of Abraham's mouth than Pedro obliged by sliding down his tree trunk, leaving behind a sizable chunk of his right shirt sleeve.

"Oh, shit," he groaned. "Now I know I'm going to get the hell kicked out of me."

"Look at the bright side." Johnny attempted reassurance. "At least it ain't your whole arm hung up there with your finger pointing the way."

Pedro grinned. "Yeah, heck. What's a hunk of sleeve?"

"This way, fellows." Abraham pointed toward some acres of high grass. "Come on, it will hide us."

"There they go. Right into the high grass." Troop Leader Allen, Jr., lowered his binoculars. "Boy, what dum-dums. Don't they know what's waiting for them in the Jersey swamps. This way," Jimmy commanded. "We'll cut around and head them off at the pass."

Now both hunted and hunters were in the full spirit of the chase. The high grass turned out to be swamp grass, three times as tall as the tenderfeet. It was chock full of gnats, mosquitoes, and bugs, buzzing, biting and breeding.

The hunted found themselves in water that was ankle deep with the imminent threat of being much deeper. In short, they were in the belly of some bad Jersey marshlands.

"Hey, man. Can anybody see where we're going?" Johnny moaned.

Panic crept in. Somebody had to pay for the trio's unfortunate situation, and poor Abraham who had led them into the grass was the logical brunt for their agonies.

"Oh, Jesus!" Pedro looked sharply at Abraham. "I got some bugs up my nose." His forefinger went frantically after the insects.

"They're coming up through my shorts," yelled Johnny, going into a St. Vitus dance.

Abraham's skin was quickly turning into pointed volcanic craters. He was slapping himself silly.

"We're lost! We're lost! Damnit, we're lost!" Pedro's voice was stuck on one note.

"Read the compass, bro," Johnny suggested desperately.

Pedro answered painfully. "The needle is shaking and pointing north."

Johnny blurted out, "Man, it always points

north. We keep going north and we're bound to hit something."

"Didn't Jimmy tell us to keep going southeast?" questioned Pedro.

Nobody remembered. Memories were blanked out by growing terror.

"Let's head north," Abraham suggested again. "That's where everybody heads for in the flicks."

They all agreed—north it was.

Way above the tall grass, perched on a slight cliff, the trackers waited. Each took turns watching through the binoculars the plight of the three *amigos*.

Although it was well past high noon, the hot sun continued to beat down without mercy. Pedro's shoes were filled to brimming with dark, thick, oozy mud while his body was gritty with grime. His courage was shaken under a mountain of fast-growing fears.

"Let's send up a smoke signal," he volunteered.

Abraham vetoed the idea in a voice strangely calm.

"Point one—no dry twigs. Point two—even if we could start a fire, we could get burned if the wind blows wrong. Better just start yelling our freaking heads off."

Three stricken throats yelled, screamed, and howled wolf patrol calls all the way to heaven.

Resting comfortably in the shade, the hunters' ears suddenly perked up at the cries of distress that came rolling in like waves.

"I think they're in trouble," said Troop Leader Allen nonchalantly, pushing off the feeling that the trio might be drowning as well as being eaten alive by piranha mosquitoes.

"We've got to help them," said a tracker tenderfoot. "It really might be serious."

Repeated sounds of "Help! Help!" like a phonograph needle stuck in a groove reinforced his concern.

Pedro shouted to Johnny and Abraham. "*Oye,* I got an idea. Let's throw up our hats. Each one throws his hat up one second after the other, like an SOS. Get it?"

Soon their round ranger hats were sailing like flying saucers up into the air from the bowels of the green swamps. Jimmy, through his binoculars, immediately identified the UFOs as boy scout hats.

"They're taunting us, hoping we'll follow and then no doubt they'll circle back, leaving us to search fruitlessly while they return to home base."

"You sure?" questioned one of the hunters, a thirteen year old with a fine analytical mind. "Jersey swamps are notorious for their stagnant waters and millions of insects, totally hostile to any intruder."

"Hummh," intoned Jimmy. "You may be right. Somebody just tossed their shoes into the air. Men,"—he paused for effect—"it's our duty as scouts to rescue them and besides," he added professionally, "it's sure to get us a rescue merit badge."

"No doubt they'll need medical attention," added a second scout.

"We may even have to make litters to carry them back to camp," added a third. "That's some more merit badges."

While all the merit badges were being mentally earned, Pedro, Johnny, and Abraham, in the middle of the hot, sticky, bug-ridden swamp, fought valiantly not to lose heart. Johnny came up with another idea.

"Let's climb on each other's shoulders and together we will be at least fifteen feet tall. You be top man, Abraham. Your face is the worst mess. This way we can get our bearings."

Abraham attempted a smile. "Gotcha. Will do."

The trackers were startled when a red blotchy

face arose like a banshee shoulders-high above the swamp grass. Abraham was waving his arms high above his head, more in supplication to the heavens than to anyone on earth, while trying to keep his balance.

"There they are," yelled Jimmy. "Wave, men. Let them know we've seen them."

The scouts sent up a din that fairly shook the Jersey everglades. Abraham, overjoyed at being discovered, began to bounce all around, causing all three of them to come tumbling down.

Ten minutes later, the hunters had found them and led them to solid ground. The three, completely covered with a natural mud pack, were indistinguishable from one another, except that Abraham could be recognized by his blue eyes. Johnny and Pedro, with some effort at boy scout discipline, identified themselves.

"Okay, boys. Now lay still. Don't move," Jimmy ordered. " 'Cause we don't know the full extent of your injuries."

"Why can't we just wash ourselves off and then get something for our bites? We got no fractures," said Pedro.

"Yeah." Abraham groaned. "There's nothing fractured except maybe our break with the scouts."

"I'm not hurt bonewise, either." Johnny moaned. "I'm just itchy, wet, tired, and getting madder every minute. Nothing like this ever happened to me in El Barrio and, believe me, that can be dangerous living, too."

"Now, now. Just take it easy." Jimmy soothed them, not about to be cheated out of the glory of rescuing three survivors of the Jersey swamps.

The rescuers began cutting down sturdy saplings, which was only permitted in case of emergencies. From these, they fashioned six long poles into makeshift stretchers. The boys were stripped of their shirts and trousers to provide support and were made to lie down on separate stretchers. Jimmy, pulling rank, ordered them not to move because mosquito poison could travel like cobra venom through their blood stream. Seeing Pedro's arm with its torn sleeve, Jimmy tied his blue bandana in a sling around Pedro's arm.

"My arm ain't broken," protested Pedro.

"Slows down the poison traveling through your system."

This act inspired the other trackers to offer not only bandanas but their white handkerchiefs for use by anyone with bug-infested noses. Johnny was the first to grab one.

In single file with Jimmy leading the procession, the rescue team made its way back to camp. The Great March was working out to be everything any scout could ever hope for. Cheers for heroes greeted them. The rescuers proudly carried the three stretchers, rejecting any offers of help with a gesture of "keep away." When Jimmy finally did speak, it was simply to say, "It's okay, scouts. I can manage."

El Supremo appeared on the scene and immediately took charge over his megaphone. Taking a swig out of his canteen, he bounced orders all over the woods in multiquadriphonics.

Buckets of icy cold brook water were poured on caked bites to cleanse them of thick layers of mud that had sun-hardened to adobe. Globs of oozy white ointment were liberally applied while the uniforms, a mass of wet muddy lumps, were removed from the improvised stretchers.

Under the watchful eye of *El Supremo,* some merit-hungry scouts washed the uniforms and hung them on poles to dry by the fire. But they were too close to the flames.

Pedro, Johnny, and Abraham, horrified, watched their Troop 633, Wolf Patrol uniforms burn so brightly that they seemed to have been dipped in the sun. Eager scouts knocked each other out to squelch the fire. But all their efforts were in vain. All that was left were smoldering blackened embers and red-hot boy scout buttons.

"What in hell. . . !" *El Supremo* choked.

The fire-fighting scouts melted away into the darkening afternoon with heavy forebodings that they would never rise above the rank of tenderfoot. By contrast, the sun was shining brightly for Jimmy Allen and his noble trackers. They relived and recounted their deeds, which became more heroic with each retelling.

"Will you check out them phonies. Taking credit for doing more when it was really less," said Johnny.

"They're blowing the action out of proportion," added Abraham, in utter disbelief.

The sun began slipping behind some tall trees, changing its many colors into one gentle orange sunset. Wrapped in heavy camping blankets, Pedro, Johnny, and Abraham huddled around a small fire. Meanwhile, the camp was busy preparing for the evening meal: a second round of franks, beans, and cocoa. The campfires had turned the green woods into a forest of multicolored flares and dancing shadows.

After dinner, the tribulations of the day were

temporarily forgotten in the singing and story-telling around the campfire.

Eventually, the crackling fires and the snoring of boy scouts blended with the breezes rustling through the leaves of high trees.

Sunrise was heralded by a skinny First Class scout who blew reveille on his bugle with the force of a hurricane. The three boys, after a long night of scratching, tossing, and turning, had fallen into an early morning sleep that bordered on a coma. Only after much prodding from Troop Leader Allen were they able to open their swollen eyes.

"Here's your shoes, fellows." Jimmy smiled. "And—er—we took up a collection of odds and ends for you to put on until you get home."

Without a word the trio slipped into their donated pants and shirts. Their mud-caked shoes had survived the fire but had dried stiff as adobe bricks with shoe strings. No doubt about it—the three survivors were a sorry mess. Yet no one laughed, smiled, or snickered. At least not to their faces.

Pedro, Johnny, and Abraham breakfasted on wheat cereal with evaporated canned milk, huddling together for sympathy. The bugle blew once again, followed by *El Supremo*'s voice.

"Men, by 0900, which is an hour and a half from now, we will be fully packed and ready for our trip back to our homes. I do not need to tell you all that a scout's motto, among others, is that next to Godliness is cleanliness. All refuse is to be collected. We will leave nature as clean as we found it. I don't want to see one bean lying around. Do you understand?"

A great roar of understanding went up from the scouts, punctuated by some ill winds forced out in tribute to the mountains of beans that had been digested. A far-off chorus softly sang in unison: "Beans, beans, the musical fruit. The more you eat, the more you toot."

"At 0900," the Supreme Leader continued, unaffected by the rude interruption, "the bugler will sound a 'fall in' and I want everybody in formation, neat as a whistle and sharp as a pin."

"Cripes, you two guys look terrible." Abraham smiled at Johnny and Pedro. But there was no doubt who looked the worst. Abraham, being the fairest, stood out the most. His mosquito bites were as close to a bad case of smallpox as one would want to see. From time to time, a scout would approach to offer condolences while taking advantage of the opportunity to gape at the misfortune of the three insect-ravaged heroes.

At 0900, the promised bugle blew, and Troop 633, along with other troops, lined up. *El Supremo* walked up and down inspecting the scouts. He paused in front of the bedraggled trio. The boys manfully snapped to attention.

"At ease, men." The Leader smiled. A flicker of concerned horror at the appearance of his three luckless scouts gave proof to the boys that they looked as bad as they felt.

"Huh, listen, scouts. If you want, I can arrange a ride back to New York for you all. You don't have to feel guilty about it because for sure your condition warrants it. What do you say?"

Pedro, Johnny, and Abraham faltered for a moment. But no one moved, no one wavered. Each stood stiffly at attention.

Finally Pedro broke the silence. "I think, sir, that we'll march with all the rest of the scouts."

El Supremo nodded his head. These were the kinds of scouts he was proud to lead. He took two steps backward, whipped to attention, and honored them with a sharp scout salute. The three boys saluted back smartly. For *El Supremo* to salute anyone was an unheard of honor.

Raising his megaphone to his lips, he let the rest of the world know his feelings.

"Men, what you see standing before me is a

prime example of the *esprit de corps* that makes up the unconquerable will of the Boy Scouts of America. These tenderfeet could have taken the easy way out, a ride to their very doors. But instead, they bravely chose to march back with us. Men, let's give these brave men a great big hip-hip-hurrah for courage."

"Hip-hip-hurrah! Hip-hip-hurrah!" The cheer was picked up from one troop to another until the New Jersey woods shook with a thundering ovation. The three tenderfeet graciously accepted the honor at rigid attention.

Somewhere in the background, a loud voice shouted, "Now let's hear it for the mosquitoes without whom all this would not have been possible."

A second voice shouted, "Three cheers for the three mosquiteers! Buzz-buzz-hurrah! Buzz-buzz-hurrah!"

Suddenly, hundreds of boy scouts broke rank and turned into khaki-colored giant mosquitoes. "Buzz-buzz-hurrah! Buzz-buzz-buzz-hurrah!" The buzzing was so loud that not even the Supreme Leader shouting for order could be overheard. Sheer exuberant exhaustion finally brought the roaring buzzing to an end. Order was restored and

Troop 633, along with the others, began the long march home.

At the subway station near the bridge they were all dismissed.

"Which way are you going, Abraham?" Pedro asked.

"I got to take the West Side line." Abraham managed a smile. "How about you two?"

"We gotta get to the east side. Johnny and me live right around the corner from each other."

Hundreds of scouts crowded the platform and quickly filled the train that roared in.

"Aw, let's wait for another one," said Johnny. "No use getting crushed. Right?"

"Right." The other two agreed. They were in no hurry to get home. Pedro jiggled a gum machine that had not held a stick of gum in years, while Johnny fooled around on a penny scale that couldn't tell an ounce from a pound. Abraham was quietly fighting his fingernails to keep them away from his itches. He began to scratch himself lightly, like a monkey in a cage. Pedro and Johnny followed the act, and soon the three were chattering, walking, and jumping like apes.

Abraham's train arrived first. He entered the

last car, waving to Pedro and Johnny who responded by doing an imitation of King Kong until the train was lost from view in the darkness of the subway tunnel. On the ride home they were quiet, each thinking of all the explaining they would have to do. After all, brand new uniforms cost a lot of money. At the corner of 104th Street, they parted.

"Hope you don't get your *culito* handed to you." That was Johnny's farewell.

"Same to you, *amigo.*"

Pedro made his way up the street, hugging the buildings so he wouldn't attract attention. At his stoop, he dashed into the dim darkness of the hallway and then slow as molasses climbed the steps to his door. He reached out to knock a dozen times, each time stopping short. He practiced poor excuses in a whisper to his mosquito-bitten shadow.

"I'd better tell the truth." He'd decided. "Jesus, our Father who art in Heaven . . ."

Pedro never finished his prayer. The door was opened by his brother Frankie.

"Hey, turkey. What the hell you doing out there praying your behind off. You done flipped or something?"

Pedro grinned weakly and slipped past his brother.

"Who is it?" said his mother.

"It's Pedro, Moms, back from his Big March. Christ, you look terrible . . ."

"Ah, Pedrito, did you have a good time?" His mother's voice was cheerful. "Come in, *hijo*. I'm in the kitchen."

"I'm coming, Moms." Pedro did at least sixty Hail Marys, took a deep breath, girded himself, and did a quick jump into the kitchen where his moms was cooking meat pies for the church bazaar. She looked up at him, smiled and looked away.

"My goodness, *hijo*. You look a mess. Quick, take a bath and get into some fresh clothes. Humm, I see you got some nasty mosquito bites."

"Yeah—uh—some." Pedro was amazed. Not one word asked about his brand new uniform.

"After your bath, I'll put some calamine lotion on your bites and then you can have dinner and early to bed. Did you earn many—how you call them—merit badges?"

"I don't know, Moms. I should at least get one for survival."

Later, refreshed, redressed, and relieved by the cooling effect of the calamine lotion, Pedro ate himself into a stupor. "After all, eat, drink, be merry for when Poppa comes home, I'm sure to die. Behind of mine, prepare for something not so fine."

"Eat, eat, there's plenty. I even got some of your favorite dessert, *flan de coco*."

"Ma?" Pedro's piece of pork chop stuck in his throat. "Ain't you gonna ask me where my brand new uniform is?"

"No, I already know and so does your Poppa. Your scout leader called to explain and said he would also call Johnny Cruz's parents and a boy named Abraham's family. He said to tell you that you all will be getting new uniforms, courtesy of the Boy Scouts of America."

"God," Pedro blew out softly. "Hail Marys do work."

Frankie, who had known from the git-go that Pedro was in no danger, smiled and helped himself to Pedro's French fried potatoes.

"Hey, bro. When's your next Great March?"

Pedro shot him a fierce look. "I dunno," came the reply.

"Well, check it out before, bro. I don't think your *culito* can survive another trip like the one you have just been through."

A rapid knocking at the door saved Frankie from a heavy response. Pedro opened it on a poor, sweaty Johnny Cruz who, with eyes downcast, moaned out, "Jee-sus, Pedro. I didn't have the heart to go home. I got to the stoop, thought about my folks getting a look at me, and seeing their forty bucks of uniform gone down the toilet bowl, and then I got a mental picture of me being flushed away."

"Well, well." Pedro opened the door wide. "Come on in, take a bath. I'll give you some fresh clothes. I got some good news for you. Hey, Moms. Set up a plate for another mosquiteer."

■ 2 ■

La Peseta (The Quarter)

I

A child wants to have a few *centavos* at least,
Some *dinero* to be able to go to the movies,
To be able to buy a hot dog or a *bacalaito*.
You know, things that other people
Who have wealth can enjoy.
To have some money in your pocket
That's a joy indeed.
You can go into the candy store
Instead of standing outside deciding

Whether to keep on walking
Or snatch a candy bar, very cool and undetected.

II

My father worked very hard on the WPA
Construction gang with *pick-y-pala,* shovel,
Digging very deep holes and filling them up too.
When he left for *trabajo* in the morning
He would give my mother money to buy food,
Always leaving something extra on top of the table
To make sure that we'd also have dessert.
On this day, he put one quarter, some dimes, and
a nickel,
Maybe forty-five or fifty cents, a whole lot.
I really wanted to go to that movie
With my new girlfriend named Cándida.
I looked at the money and said,
"Well, they would not miss it, you know."
So I took the quarter and put it into my socks,
Pushing it all the way down until it was under-
neath—inside my sneaker.

III

As my father started to walk out the door
To go to his job of *pick-y-pala,*
He said to my mother,

"I left some change."
And my mother said, "Bring it to me."
My father came back for the money,
And he looked and he quietly said,
"There is a quarter missing."
Oh, if he had only gone, I thought,
Then Mama would not have known a quarter was
missing.

IV

I immediately began to look all over the floor
And under the beds and over everything.
And my father just stood there,
Looking at me.
I, who always complained
About going down to the grocery store
Or even washing behind my ears,
I, who always was the last to volunteer,
Was all of a sudden so fantastically willing
To look for the missing *peseta*.

V

My father said to my sister,
"Have you seen the quarter?"
My sister said, "No."
My father said to me,

"Have you see it?"
And I said, "No, Poppa,
Can't you see I'm trying hard to find it?"
I was really wishing I had never taken
That *maldita peseta.*
I was not born a criminal,
I just wanted a chance to see what it was like
To have a quarter.

VI

My father looked at me,
And I knew that he knew
That the quarter was somewhere on me.
But not to make me feel completely guilty,
He said, "I'll frisk everybody."
Leaving me there sweating to the last—till
Finally, it was my turn.
"Let me see your pants, son."
I took them off.
He emptied my pockets
And while he was doing all this frisking,
I was loudly proclaiming my innocence complete
with crossing *corazón.*
"Poppa, how could you even think this?"
"Poppa, have you ever known me to take anything
That didn't belong to me?"

VII

While in my mind justifying it,
As part of my inheritance.
Poppa said, "Take off your sneakers."
I took my smelly sneakers off.
Poppa beat them hard against each other—
    I was so glad it wasn't my *cabeza.*
He said, "Your socks."
So I took one sock off.
The sock with the quarter was the last to go.
I slipped it off, holding the coin inside
With my thumb and forefinger,
And praying to all the Gods in Heaven
That the quarter would stay in the sock,
Which it did not.
Plink-ling-ling the quarter came tumbling out.
My face said, "How in the hell did that get there?"
I tried to smile, but that didn't work.

VIII

My father dove straight for me
As I dove under the bed.
My father could not get under it because it was a
    very low bed.
So he proceeded very calmly
To take the mattress off.

In the background, my mother seemed undecided
on child-abuse, 'cause she was saying,
"Don't hit him on the head.
Because you can make him *loco*.
If you got to hit him,
Around the legs is good enough.
Don't hit him in the head.
I want him to be *inteligente* when he grows up."
I cringed in terror—suppose Poppa broke my legs.

IX

My father ripped off the springs
And then removed his pants belt.
It looked bigger than the whip
That Zorro used to make his mark.
I broke into a run.
I became the greatest quarterback in the world.
My father went for me
And I ducked him, cut, and split,
Ran, stopped on a dime, and
Returned nine cents change.
I wondered if Poppa would believe that *peseta*
had just rolled off the table
And without me feeling a thing had slipped into
my sock and wormed its way under my foot.

X

My father came after me like Superman,
Faster than a speeding bullet, more powerful
Than a locomotive, able to leap backyard fences
In a single bound.
He was a natural-born athlete
Who played for the Cuban Stars, the Black Stars,
The Puerto Rican Stars—*Olé, olé.*
I had to beat my father running,
Because my ass depended on it.
And then— I was caught.
I tried to smile as I waited for the blows that were
    to come,
But my father just looked at me and said,
"Son, why didn't you ask for it?
I would have given it to you.
Did you have to steal it?"
I just looked at Poppa and began to cry.
My sorry tears ran down my cheeks.
I just stood there feeling like a chump.
What can a guy say at a time like that?

▪ 3 ▪
The Konk

When I was a kid, many folks spent a lot of time, effort, and money trying to pass for white. Very few homes did not have some kind of skin-bleaching cream. If poverty prevented its purchase, raw lemon juice would suffice. Cream or juice was liberally applied to the skin with the hope of turning it yellow, which was light, if not white.

Parents were constantly pinching the noses of their children so that flat, wide nostrils could be unnaturally forced into sculptured images of white folks' noses.

Running neck and neck were hair-straightening and coloring effects. The very poor made up batches of Vaseline, lye, and harsh brown Octagon soap for their hair-straightening. For those who could afford it, there were jars of heavy white cream with "You too can have beautiful hair" advertised on the label.

Even more money could buy a marcel, which straightened curly hair by pressing it out with iron-hot combs after dipping one's head in oil. The smell of burnt hair often overpowered the odors of garbage-littered alleyways. Even comic books carried ads for beauty care. One could earn a Red Ryder B.B. rifle or a bicycle if one sold enough of a particular brand of lightening cream.

By the time I was fourteen, I had grown tired of my curly hair being called "nappy," *pasas* (raisins), or *pelo malo* (bad hair). One day I decided to take the plunge. I went to a barber shop way up in the wilds of the South Bronx, recommended by some walking exponents of one hair-straightening process known as the "konk."

At Prospect Avenue station, I made my exit and headed for the barbershop, located on Westchester Avenue. A huge sign in the window advertised its specialty.

The Konk

ROY'S BARBER SHOP—HAIR STRAIGHTENED
KONKS—FIVE DOLLARS—SATISFACTION
GUARANTEED

Overcoming my hesitancy, I marched into that barber shop like I copped konks every day. On the walls were photographs of all kinds of celebrities, including fighters like Kid Gavilan and Ray Robinson. They flashed big smiles signifying their joy at sporting straight hair via konks or marcels.

Some sad blues were being wailed by Billie Holiday from an antique radio. I figured Billie was saying konking was all right too. Two young black men wearing white barbershop jackets were playing checkers. One of them looked at me with a smile and in singsong asked, "What will it be, li'l brother? A trim trip or the works?"

"Gimme a konk," I said, as if I'd invented the word.

"Sit right there, li'l brother." He pointed to a mid-Victorian barbershop chair. "We'll get you straightened out in no time at all."

With cool-breeze apprehension, I lightly eased myself into the chair, which in my vivid imagination resembled the hot seat at Sing Sing.

"I'm Roy, bro. What's yours?"

"Mine's Piri," I answered, my eyes glued to his own natural unprocessed hair.

Roy put on some rubber gloves like doctors use when they have to touch something they don't really want to.

"Umhh." He frowned. "This won't do . . . won't do at all."

I wondered if my Puerto Rican hair was going to be left out of konk, too. "What's the matter?"

"Too much grease, son. You got grease on your head that's been there from the year one. Gotta give you an A-1 shampoo first, okay? It's $2.50 extra."

Too deeply involved by now to say no, I agreed and Roy proceeded to do his art. After the final rinsing, he squeaked my hair between his thumb and forefinger. "It's clean now."

I had to admit my curly hair had not looked that clean in a long time. Seeing my reflection in the mirror, I grunted approval.

Roy examined my scalp carefully, arousing my anxiety.

"You got lots of good hair to work with."

I bubbled with pleasure. At last my hair pleased somebody even if it were just for a konk. Roy took out a huge jar of Dixie Peach Hair Pomade. He plunged his right hand in and came out with a gigantic blob of its thick yellow substance. I staggered under its weight as he worked close to a pound into my hair.

"Man, you sure are heavy on that grease," I protested.

"Got to, li'l man, cause without the Dixie Peach, the konk can burn your scalp right off your head. In fact, bro, it can cause your hair to fall right off your head or turn it red along with your scalp."

"Jesus Christ," I said, forcing my voice to stay without panic. Like I never thought it was going to be dangerous.

"A lot of bad can happen if it's not done right." My artist brother droned on confident in his art. "If you want white man's hair, there's a price you gotta pay. Whatcha say? Now's the time to stop or go."

I smiled bravely and said, "Go, bro. But say, man. How come you don't konk your hair, seeing as you're in the business."

Roy just mumbled, "No way, man. Konks or marcels ain't my stick. I just do it for others 'cause it's part of my living wages."

Satisfied that my head was greased to his satisfaction, Roy unscrewed the top of a large blue jar. I observed a soft whitish cream that smelled like sulphuric acid. With a comb, he began working it into my curly, terror-stricken, cringing hairs.

"Now, li'l brother, relax and listen. Soon as you start feeling your scalp begin burning, just gimme a holler. I sure don't want to be responsible for your hair turning red, let alone dropping out. Don't get scared if you just feel your scalp warming up. That's just the konk doing its thing. Only holler when it really starts to burn. Some scalps are tender, others can. . . ."

Just then a voice interrupted from the doorway. "Good morning, gentlemen. Anybody feeling lucky today?"

In the mirror, I saw a boy. He was a numbers runner just a few years older than my fourteen, high yellow of color with soft reddish natural brown hair. He thoughtfully checked out my reflection, his eyes glued compassionately to the top of my head, by now a smoldering mass of plaster of Paris.

The smell of burning, agonizing hair permeated the barber shop. I strained my neck out with a grin after what seemed like hours instead of minutes. "Hey, man. My hair is starting to burn."

Damnit. I wasn't being heard. Roy the artful barber was too busy checking out the numbers game.

"Yeah, I sure feel lucky today. Gimme 50¢ on 347, 50¢ on 656, and a buck combination on 437."

"Hey, man. My head's burning."

If he refused to hear me, he should at least be able to smell the smoke. I waited coolly as I could for a couple of more suffering seconds and then without any kind of embarrassment began to let out all kinds of yells.

"Hey, man. I ain't shitting. My head's on fire."

"Listen, George," Roy went on rapping to the young numbers runner, "I guess that's all for now. No, wait, George, hold on. Gimme 50¢ on 333. I really feel lucky today."

I wished I felt that lucky. I was already heading for the faucet with my head on fire. Roy finally got hip to the seriousness of the situation and got to the sink with me.

Attempting to comfort me, he said, "It's supposed to burn a little. You want it to come out cool, don't ya?"

He brought the three-alarm fire that was my scalp under control by life-saving, cold-water rinsing. He toweled my hair dry. I stared into the mirror amazed. My short coils of curls no longer than a couple of inches around my ears were now a waterfall of hair, dead straight and hanging limply down to my shoulders.

Roy combed while I inwardly swore I looked like Cochise, if not Prince Valiant.

"Now for a hair cut, bro. Do you want it long or short?"

"Long, man," I said. "Long enough for a pompadour in front and a duck's ass in the back."

"Gotcha."

Snip, snip, snip. Comb, comb, comb. Clip, clip, clip.

Straight razor, sweet-smelling hair lotion, some more combing, a pat here, a pat there.

"Okay, man. That's it. You got a Roy Special. Hey, man, open your eyes. Check yourself out."

Roy's voice sounded so pleased that I opened them in good faith. I ran my fingers through my hair. It was like fine silk. Roy expertly brushed away loose hairs and with a final flourish liberally splashed me with fragrant after-shave lotion. He held up a large mirror in back of me, which allowed me to see in my reflection the glory of his work.

Good God Almighty! I was sure looking good. I now had the biggest, softest, silkiest pompadour in the whole world and a duck ass style that would force vain ducks to drown themselves in sheer envy.

"Compliments of the house, li'l brother," Roy

said, handing me a long slim-jim barber's comb that a short while back could only have been used to comb my eyebrows.

"Gee, thanks, man." I combed my hair in the mirror just like the cat going to the electric chair in the film *Knock On Any Door*.

"What's the tab, bro?"

"Five dollars, li'l brother, plus $2.50 for A-1 Shampoo."

I gave him $9.50; the extra two was to cover some inner shame I was somehow feeling.

"Thank you, bro." Roy saluted me.

George smiled friendly at me as I walked toward the door.

"Feeling lucky today? I always pay off, so no worries."

"Yeah," I said. "Gimme a dime on 692."

I didn't check his face out. A dime is pretty cheap. But how was he to know my hair konk had damn near broken me financially.

Roy called out some last minute professional advice.

"Hey, li'l brother. Don't forget you gotta keep the treatment up or your hair will definitely return to its nappy self."

"Yeah, sure," I called back, moving fast away from Roy's Barber Shop. I began checking myself out in store windows, combing and recombing my newly reconstructed hair. I dropped my comb more than once—bending over mussed up hair, providing another excuse to recomb it.

Going home, I purposely rode between the rumbling cars of the subway train so that the blast of air caused my new hair to rise and fly. It was no longer bound to the greasy gravity of Dixie Peach.

Leaving the train at 103rd Street, I walked into my block of 104th Street where most everybody knew me. Heads began snapping my way, and smiles grew into jeering shouts of "Hey, monkey, what's that shit on your haid?" One renamed me "Konko Pete" on the spot, followed by "Just wait until your hair turns red and your scalp drops dead."

I really felt like punching the insulters out but cooled the idea as being suicidal. I couldn't fight a whole block. As I climbed the stairs to my apartment, I braced myself for whatever else was ahead. I paused a long second outside my door and then strolled in, hoping no one would notice me. My two brothers were busy playing a card game of knuckles. My sister was into her Wonder Woman comics. They looked up at me vaguely, but it was enough for them to spot my new hair style. I dared them with my eyes to say anything that would put me down.

My brothers kept quiet although bursting to laugh. My sister, however, could not contain herself, blurting out, "*Mira, mira.* Piri's got a wig."

"Wig, shit," I snarled. "This ain't no wig. This here is my new hair."

There was no way my brothers could contain themselves any longer. Their laughter came out roaring like wheels on a subway train. Tears of rage mixed with embarrassment jumped out of my eyes. I wished the living room floor would swallow me up.

I hit out at Ray, causing my hair to come trembling down over my face. Their laughter increased. All I could do was stand there with my new straight hair stuck like wires of black spaghetti to my angry, sweaty face.

The noise brought in Momma, followed by Poppa still chewing on his supper. Suddenly everybody was silent. I walked slowly over to the sofa and plunked down heavily on it, feeling old and tired at fourteen and wondering why my strong young legs refused to hold me up.

Poppa shook his head. He knew what my hurting was all about. Momma sat down by my side and caressed my wilted, abused hair. Then hugging me close, she allowed my tears of hurt and shame to be absorbed by her big momma breasts. She whispered to me, "*Hijo,* what have you done to your beautiful hair?"

"Oh, Moms," I whispered back. "I just didn't want to be different any more. I'm so tired of being called names. I ain't no raisinhead or nothing like that."

Momma hugged me very closely and said out loud, "Don't you ever be ashamed of being you. You want to know something, *negrito.* I wouldn't trade you for any *blanquitos.*"

The next day found me playing stick ball with a red bandana around my forehead, sporting the baldest head in town.

▪ 4 ▪
Mighty Miguel

Miguel Suarez, at fourteen, had an incredible imagination which, without effort, could take him into any dimension he wished. He could be a bearded pirate of the past leading his men into battle against Spanish galleons or a space pilot of the future zooming through outer space at supersonic speeds, exploring unknown universes.

Other boys and girls wanted to be definite things like engineers, pilots, lawyers, doctors, or teachers. But Miguel wanted to be an imaginer, a dreamer, who out of fantasies and illusions could create a reality for himself. A few people understood Miguel's world. Others just shook their heads wondering if he was all there.

When Miguel was ten years old, he had suffered an attack of polio, which at first confined him to a wheelchair. But Miguel practiced walking every day, a few feet at a time. After four years, he was able to move about quite cheerfully without anyone's help, even climbing stairs.

"Some day," Miguel said, "I will climb a high mountain and sing me a song from way up on top and show all the world what happens when one doesn't doubt one's dreams."

One lovely summer evening, Miguel's parents were going out to the theatre. As usual, they asked their neighbor, Mrs. González, to check out their son from time to time. If Miguel needed her, he could call on the phone. His parents had told him that they would be back late and not to stay up waiting.

Miguel glanced at his watch, which said half-past eight—twilight time. He had grown tired of reading and watching television and was debating whether to call Mrs. González to invite her over for a game of chess. He decided not to since she was well into her seventies and needed her rest. From his third floor bedroom, he gazed thoughtfully out into the backyard of the family's brownstone.

Night was gently falling in harmony with a pale moonlight. Miguel reached over to the dresser and brought back a bag of jelly beans. Munching a mouthful, he fought off feeling lonely. From his armchair by the window, he studied the backyards below, tinged with bright lights and strange shadows from other houses.

Slowly, his eyes began to close, his head lolling into a sleepy nod. Suddenly, he sensed a movement outside in the darkness. His interest aroused, he allowed one eye to open just a little, for sleep was really on his mind. Nothing moved. So his eye began to close again.

Soon he heard tinkling laughter, rising and falling with childlike joy. Both his eyes popped open. Straining his vision toward the sounds, he made out a marble statue of a young maiden, sculptured in true Greek fashion, set on top of a water fountain.

The young maiden's head was slightly tilted, both marble hands holding a large gourd from which cascades of water poured without end. Nothing appeared to move except a backyard squirrel Miguel had named Oscar. The moon went behind a night cloud, and Miguel's vision was now a blur of outlined form. Oscar was chattering away in disgust about the shortage of good food. Miguel being of a kind nature sent out a message in perfect squirrel language that brought Oscar scurrying his way to receive a baker's dozen worth of king-sized jelly beans.

Thanking Miguel profusely, courteous even with his squirrel mouth full, he did his best to repay the kindness by five minutes worth of bushy tail fanning to ease the hot summer air away. Then with a flourish of his most magnificent tail, he gave Miguel a last look as he sailed out the window, headed for his tree, among the largest to grow in Brooklyn.

The moon finally got rid of the dark night cloud blocking its lovely light. Lo and behold! The marble maiden was moving. Miguel saw she was looking directly at him. A wide smile spread over her face while her two marble eyes blinked, flashing yellow pinpoints of light his way.

Miguel made a funny face by wiggling his nose at the maiden, who tossed her head and began to sing softly a song about love. The backyard was filled with her bell-like sound. She even did a graceful dance, delicately perched on the edge of her marble fountain, pausing every so often to wink flirtatiously at Miguelito.

One might suppose that Miguel would have been taken aback. It is not every day that a statue tries to make hay. But Miguel had survived heavier adventures in countless trips through imagination's gates.

He had seen three-headed Grookers on Venus that were horrid to behold with thirty-three arms coming out of each of their shoulders. They enjoyed licking their unfortunate victims after first wrapping them in different flavored licorice sticks.

There were adventures on Jupiter where gravity proved so great that only the foul-smelling Jellions could exist—except for Miguelito, of course. Not to forget the Treetons from the planet Treet, who were similar to King Kong, only seven times bigger. Although bald-headed, their bodies were covered with a purple fuzz that shimmered like velvet. They also had eyes all over their bodies, which blinked on and off like Christmas lights. They were as large as the Goofsters from the planet Goofus were small.

The Goofsters strained out their victims' brains and cast away the empty remains, which were quickly devoured by the six-headed Skeevies, who ate anything except themselves. Being utterly repulsive, they would puke up if they ate each other by mistake.

Miguel had seen plenty of dangers. Maybe he was a little nervous at times, but mostly he was cool and calm. At the last moment before immediate death, he would somehow be saved. After all, it was all in his mind.

Three weeks ago, he had taken a voyage to the center of Uranus via a light ship, right in the middle of his math teacher's dronings. Mr. Número had no imagination to make math lessons interesting. So Miguel drifted away in the temple of his mind. The multibrained Antocpluses were like giant ants with butterfly wings who added and multiplied themselves from flames, subtracting and dividing only when necessary for survival. He was almost being devoured by these creatures when he was jolted back to reality by Mr. Número, who could never figure Miguel out.

In retrospect, Miguel decided that he had not been in danger because he had a counterweapon to the Antocpluses. It was his Buck Rogers water blaster, a weapon that the Antocpluses feared as much as Miguel's water hand grenades made from 100% fireproof balloons. But the marble statue was something else. Miguel stared keenly at her face. She winked a great big smile, blew him a kiss, and thereupon turned back into marble stone, leaving Miguel quite alone.

He began to feel a bit thirsty from eating too many jelly beans, so he decided to make his way down to the kitchen on the first floor. Reaching the second floor landing, he caught sight of an ancient being with creaking bones and wrinkled skin. The apparition was an old woman, swinging along real cool. She was dressed in a short mini skirt and a deep cut peasant blouse. Her bony knees were clicking like castanets, while her rickety ankles trembled precariously on six-inch French high heels. She wore her sparse gray hair in a pony tail and for beauty's sake, a huge sunflower right behind her left ear. From time to time, she would pluck out a few sunflower seeds and chew away.

Sighting Miguel, she glanced at him in a most coquettish way, flashing surprisingly long eyelashes, which Miguelito suspected were falsies. He acknowledged her greeting and continued down the last flight of stairs.

In the dining room, a host of multicolored flaming eyeballs rose in a swarm from the dining room table, buzzing furiously. When Miguel snapped on the light, they disappeared amidst a great wail of anguish. Thinking the matter over, he snapped the light switch off, bringing the eyeballs back into view once more. This time the glaring pupils were more kindly disposed as they stared at Miguel. Some even winked. They were not naturally mean. But they could only see in the dark and could not stand the light.

Miguel chuckled to himself. It had really been a long time since he had naturally tripped out in his own *casa.* In the kitchen, he took a quart of milk from the refrigerator and poured himself a large glass. He was reaching for his favorite cookies when he heard a voice at his elbow.

"Pardon me, sweetie, but you are in my way."

Miguel turned and to his amazement, a most grotesque figure stood before him. It was red all over, with a semblance of human shape, except that it had two horns on its forehead and a long pointed tail. A mustache and Vandyke beard topped it off.

Miguel blurted out loud, "Christ Almighty. You sure look like *El Diablo* himself."

"Right you are, dearie," the Devil said. "You get a red star for that. Now, pardon me. You are in my way. I've got to get the dishes done, if you don't mind."

The ugliness tied a bright red apron around its pot-bellied middle, carefully putting on waterproof gloves that reached to its elbows, and strolled over to the sink. In answer to Miguel's astonishment, the creature, snorting smoke said, "What's the matter, honey? Ain't you ever seen the Devil before?"

"Jesus," thought Miguel. "And all these years I've been afraid of you. Just wait till I get the word out to the world that you're really just a *veguila* guy."

Loaded up with his glass of milk and lots of Oreo cookies, Miguel excused himself and left the kitchen. Mellow sounds were emanating from the hallway. Six pink-cheeked cherubs were performing a Gregorian chant, accompanied by Fluid Fingers Louie on his golden electric harp and Sweet Lips Gabriel doing a sensual thing on his silver-toned French horn. Miguel listened for a wonderful minute to the beauty of the music and the chorus. He smiled at them in appreciation and left a few Oreo cookies to share whenever a five-minute break time came around.

Finishing his glass of milk and cookies, Miguel glanced into the living room, which faced the street side of the brownstone. The sofa and heavy wooden coffee table had been placed up against one wall leaving the larger part of the floor space empty. The blue Turkish rug had been rolled up and moved out of the room. The numerous hanging plants in brightly colored rope holders were swaying to the strains of a Latin hustling soul. Three-inch fireflies flickered here and there, moonlighting as night club lights, thus giving the entire large room a mood of candlelight softness.

Out of nowhere appeared Minni the Crone who was doing a professional version of the latest hustle steps with the Devil. Their timing was perfect, their number was together. No step was too difficult for them to execute. They danced all over the floor, walls, and ceiling of the room. Not even gravity could stop their dancing genius. Miguel watched them in silence, mouth wide opened, most impressed.

"Wow!" he exclaimed at last. "You two should really have your own TV Saturday night special."

"And on prime time without a doubt," the Devil shyly agreed.

"Do you really think we're that good?" purred Minni, knowing full well they were that and better.

They glided into a bossa nova hustle, without missing a breath or whisper of the music's sounds, which steadily were growing into a hypnotic crescendo. The plants swung in crazy rhythm to the music, while the fireflies did a lighting job that would have honored any top Broadway hit.

Minni danced with abandon, throwing herself with great passion into the arms of her dancing companion. Seared by her sudden show of emotion, the Devil turned shy and moved away from her reach. Undaunted, Minni swung into a boss samba all by herself without missing a beat.

The evening air was becoming more and more humid, Miguel was sweating most profusely, his head now filled with refreshing thoughts of a nice cool shower. Minni digging that Miguel was planning to leave, gyrated her body faster than a belly dancer trying to recapture his interest. All she succeeded in doing was shaking loose her giant sunflower from behind her right ear, causing it to crash painfully on her tender toes.

Receiving no sympathy from the Red Devil or Miguel, she picked up her giant sunflower and, holding it like a machine gun, began spraying them with a barrage of seeds. Checking out that Miguel was enjoying it, she ceased her crossfire. His mouth was as big as a toy balloon and his pockets were almost as full. Chomping happily on organic sunflower seeds, he fairly flew up the two flights of stairs with the added energy.

In the bathroom, he undressed and stepped under the shower. The cold blast of water sent his imagination to the planet Raina, where life was always wet and nobody had ever thought to invent an umbrella until Miguel. He had fashioned an umbrella by weaving it out of the giant leaves from the water plums, which were as big as pumpkins. The Rainees became Driees overnight. They learned to make umbrellas by the millions and built houses that grew into green mansions. Miguel was made a deity, but he never returned because he had heard that after a year of being dry, the Rainees had turned to powder and were all blown away. Miguel had made an oath never again to meddle with a planet's natural evolution.

Finishing his shower, he went back to his bedroom, tired but content. It had been a long day's journey into sleeping time. Miguel eased himself into his bed, welcoming the comforts of his familiar mattress.

Suddenly, he was startled to realize he was not alone. Minni the Crone was sharing the bed with him.

"Oh," was all Miguel could say, hastily covering up all the way to his chin.

Minni took his response as a sign of welcome. She sat up in bed, her clothes lying in a sloppy mess on the chair next to the window. Miguel's blush set his nose to twitching. He felt himself blush from something else beside the summer heat.

Pointing a long gnarled finger at him, Minni accused him. "You copped out at the last, *mon amour*. You left me hanging flat on a high note. As for that red fool, he sure ain't no *caballero*."

She fluttered her false eyelashes coyly. Miguel's embarrassment continued to grow. At that moment, he perceived some strange rumblings coming from his closet. Glad for any distractions, he wrapped his sheet around him and yanked open the closet door.

Huddled deep within its narrow interior was the Devil. Miguel shook his head in plain disgust.

"Shame on you, man. What are you? Some kind of peeping Tom? Boy, you really need to have your values uplifted."

Minni did not wait to hear any explanation from the Devil. She had no wish to mess with him any more. Hastily, she put on her mini skirt and peasant blouse and slipped into her six-inch French heels. Stumbling a bit, she flung herself out of the open window.

Miguel, followed by the Devil, peeked cautiously out the window, expecting to see the splattered remains of Minni down below. Instead, she lay quietly on her back, every inch the lady, popping sunflower seeds like there was no *mañana.* Miguel studied her for a while, relieved that she was not hurt. He liked her, but only as a friend.

Gazing briefly at the starlit night, Miguel was lost for a while in thought. Withdrawing from the window, he stretched mightily, crashing face to face with the Red Devil.

"God in Heaven, *carajo!*" Miguel was bombed out of his mind by a murderous gas attack loaded with a solid garlic front. He choked out tearfully, "You're as bad as the hongree Lenas, the hybrid hyenas of the rotten planet of Fooey. Their breath is lousy too."

Miguel coughed up a breeze, his eyes tearing. *El Diablo* did his best to apologize for his lack of good taste. With just the right touch of dramatic embarrassment, he lowered his head in shame. His long red tail, with a heart for an arrow on the end, was thumping away, begging forgiveness. Not buying the act, Miguel dove for his water blaster.

The Red Devil backed away, panic-stricken, to seek refuge under Miguelito's bed. Unfortunately, the space was too small for him, and he found himself scrunched in two at the waist, tight as a drum. Realizing he was trapped, the Devil lost his cool and became quite the hysterical fool.

Miguel bounced up and down on the his bed a couple of times. As far as he was concerned, this was an open-and-shut case of peeping tomism with bad breath compounding the felony.

"Oh, Miguelito," *El Diablo* pleaded his case. "I cleaned the kitchen and scrubbed the floor. I even made you a turkey salad for your lunch tomorrow. Now you got to admit that's positive. I did take the liberty of helping myself to a little snack of hot sausages on burned toast and some red hot peppers imported from your most beautiful island of Puerto Rico. And one delicious glass of warm olive oil from Spain—you know, Puerto Rico's mother country."

"No way," snapped Miguel. "Spain ripped us off. No real mother would do that."

"Well, then, *amiguito*. I hope you're not angry about the dancing. There's really nothing between Minni and me. We two are certainly not meant for each other."

Miguel maintained his ice cold silence. The Devil's mind raced for some further plea to ameliorate his punishment. Miguel bounced on him half a dozen times just to show he was still listening.

"Ain't there no way I can be saved? Hellalujah. Hellalujah. Ain't there no one can show me the way?"

"Okay, brother. I'm ready to show you the way. But first of all, it is HAL-LE-LU-JAH!" Miguel punctuated his spelling lesson with a hit to the Devil's head. Taking care to be cautious, Miguel questioned him. "Are you asking for salvation for real or are you using redemption for a cover, like maybe an excuse to escape?"

A quick hurt look spread red over the Devil's face.

"Diggit, man. I'm real for salvation whatever it takes." He quickly replaced his hurt feelings with an angelical smile that spread over every inch of his face.

"When I get out of here, I will preach the good word. If Saul became Paul, why can't *El Diablo* become God?"

Realizing he had made a serious *faux pas,* the Devil tried to silence his big mouth.

" 'Cause," Miguel reminded him, gently guiding the lost lamb, "that's what got your *culito* kicked out of heaven in the first place. Your rotten memory is bound to get you in trouble again."

The Devil redeemed himself by making the

sign of the cross as neatly as any pope. Miguel's water blaster was pushed even tighter against *El Diablo*'s nose, flattening its aquiline structure. Stalling for time, the Red Peril blurted out, "Man, did I ever tell you the story about what really went down with J.C.'s birth? Listen, kid, it seems that an immaculate conception was really in doubt on account of . . ."

Miguel bounced down so hard the Devil's chin blended in with the bedroom floor. He roared, "Damn, don't you get blasphemous with me or, by God, I'll blast you to hell."

"Could you please put that in writing?" came back a small voice. Great expectations began popping like pimples all over the Devil's slickster face.

"I'll do better than that." Miguel took a calculated steady aim with his H_2O controls set at maximum destruction right at the *diabilito*'s forehead.

"I might as well end this stalemate one way or the other." Miguel's eyes turned upward. "Lord, forgive me for what I am about to do."

"No, no, not that way. Let's do it the nonviolent way," screamed *El Diablo*. *"Coño,* my soul is truly yearning for the goodness of salvation."

From under the bed, his squeaky voice rang out, "I ask that you all bear witness that I dearly wish to repent."

Miguel stared dead center at the Red Mess for a long moment.

"Listen, mac, I think you're just lying. So get ready for game time. Uh, do you wanna blindfold?"

The Devil's eyes were frozen to Miguelito's finger tightening a killer hair trigger.

"Easy there, brother. Listen, couldn't we discuss salvation a bit better if I were out from under the bed? We'd certainly be in a better position to see things eye to eye. Christ, will you look at me! Scrunched all up with my poor nose taking a beating from my rotten smelling toes."

The red fellow's nose quivered in disgust. He even threw in a gagging or two hoping to elicit some Christian compassion from holy Miguel.

"Naw, talk from there," said Miguel, wise to the Devil's ways from having attended many a Sunday school lesson.

"I know about your reputation. You're nothing but a dirty-dealing, no-account, back-stabbing, flea-bitten, bushwacking, king-sized liar, and no ways to be trusted."

Miguelito leaped high in the air and came

down with a terrible thump. *El Diablo*'s breath was forced out of him, so it took a while for him to regain his composure. After a minute, he regained his self-control and in a voice as sweet as honeysuckle, whispered, "Since you know so much about me, then it stands to reason that you also know that I was once called Lucifer, Bearer of Light. You gotta know that I was God's number one right-hand person."

"Yeah, but you weren't satisfied with that. You tried to take over, strong-arm no doubt. You just hadda be number one, no matter what."

"Aw shoot!" the Devil protested. "I ain't the only one to think that way. If you're gonna be somebody, then be number one. You gotta admit that makes sense."

"Only if you don't step all over people along the way. Just because it's being done, don't make the thing right."

Hoping he was not being noticed, Slick Red was slowly wiggling out from under the bed. Miguel, on constant alert, did some more heavy pounding on the bed pressing Mr. Red Devil's back into a pretzel.

"Pul-eese, for God's sake, get off my case. Can't you at least rearrange your doggone weight from time to time so I can breathe a little?"

Miguel kindly shifted his weight, allowing the Devil space to pump some air into his lungs. The room smelled from a mixture of garlic and sulphuric acid, which was worse than the men's toilet in the subway. Miguel quickly reached for his bureau to find some jasmine incense. He lit several sticks hoping to take care of the *Diablo*'s dirty odors.

"No doubt you have forgotten that next to godliness is cleanliness."

The Devil's eyes were closed in deep meditation. Without opening them, he said in a matter-of-fact tone, "I've been thinking that I really ought to make a clean breast of all my past sins. May I say it in my own way on just what went down before." The Devil was cool. "I mean about . . . er . . . interrupting you and Minni."

"Go ahead, man. I'm listening, real close."

"I was peeking from the closet. But there's a good reason. I came up to your room because I heard a disturbance and I was concerned about your welfare. I didn't mean to interrupt your party."

"Are you trying to insinuate something? Come on out with it. Whatcha trying to say?" Miguel was seeing *mucho* red.

The Devil stammered a little and his red face crimsoned even more.

"Oh, well. If you don't consider sitting in bed, both of you in a state of undress something, well . . ."

Miguel was by now more than just a little disturbed by the Devil's innuendoes. The Devil, sensing he was on a dangerous track, changed his tone.

"I know, of course, that there's really nothing going on between the two of you. Minni is a very nice person, a bit overly passionate at times. But a real lady, in fact a reputation above reproach."

"She ain't bad," Miguel admitted reluctantly.

Minni's sleepy voice rose from the yard. "Thanks, loads, darlings. I knew you both really cared."

"She's just sloppy and not too polite," Miguel said, not skipping a beat.

"Oh, really." Minni moaned down below, splashing up huge tears of hurt feelings.

"I've never been so insulted in all my life. Just keep it up, Miguelito, and there's a good chance that we're never going to make it up the church aisle."

Silence followed these remarks, so Minni

quickly added, "I know you didn't mean it, Miguel. I forgive you."

Her words were reinforced by a sprinkling shower of shelled heart-shaped sunflower seeds, each wrapped in multicolored ribbons. The showering continued until the room was nearly filled up with seeded ribbons.

"Well, Minni is certainly messing up your room," said Dainty's Inferno, hoping her rating would drop.

"I don't consider my room getting messed up. I've got a real thing for sunflower seeds, and the only way I can get some from Minni is when I get her all riled up."

"You're pretty smart, *muchacho,*" admitted the long suffering *Diablo.*

After stuffing seeds into his mouth for a while, Miguel felt ready to return to the serious business of salvation. The Devil knew his moment of truth had come. He broke out in a high falsetto, "I'm redeemed by the blood of the lamb. I'm washed from sin. I am. I know I am."

Miguel respectfully interrupted. "Do you really wish for salvation?"

"Yes, yes, oh, Lordy, yes I do." *El Diablo* was responding without a moment of hesitation. "Lay it on me, brother. Hit me hard with the light. Put me on the road that's heaven-bound. Just point me toward my father's lovely green mansions."

The Devil was going through all kinds of emotional changes, puffing fire and brimstone, nearly bursting a gut trying to project an angelic image.

Feeling obligated to inquire again, Miguel asked, "Do you truly want to be saved?"

"Yes. Yes, I do, I do." The Devil wailed away.

"Okay, *Don Diablito.* I guess I believe you."

Saying this, Miguel tugged and pulled the Devil from under the bed. It took quite a while for the Red Caballero to get his disjointed figure back into its abnormal shape.

"There, there," soothed Miguel. "You're all right now."

Brushing off some popping sunflower seeds from the Devil's round shoulders, Miguel placed one hand over the red fellow's hot head.

"Kneel down and close your eyes and sort of hum 'Closer my Lord to thee.' I will baptize you until you are completely washed from your rotten sins. Come on now, kneel down."

Miguel shoved him down gently.

"Just keep meditating. Soon you'll be as white as a dove, by Jove."

The Devil was all caught up in the event. He went into a round of Hallelujahs pouring out at least seven to the second. His eyes were tightly shut in respectful reverence, forgetting completely that the magic ingredient in baptism was H_2O, one of his worst enemies.

Miguel opened up with an automatic rapid fire, emptying all his water ammunition dead straight at the reconverting Devil. Convert *número uno* opened his purple eyes just long enough for them to cross and with a parting "Amen" from Miguelito, the ex–sinner went up in a *whooossh* of smoke, entwined with dainty flames that roasted every last one of the sunflower seeds piled up in the bedroom.

"Well," thought Miguel, delightfully popping hot roasted seeds into his insatiable mouth. "I'm glad it's over. He should be arriving at his father's just about now."

Far off in the heavenly distance, Miguel heard rolling thunder mixed in with flashing lightning.

"Ummmh . . . guess he got there."

Miguel looked out the window to check out the sky, observing Minni at the same time, sleeping peacefully, no doubt dreaming of a hot torrid love affair somewhere.

Her peaceful slumbering affected Miguel. He began to stretch his arms and yawn. Once into bed he fell immediately into a gentle, well-deserved rest.

In his dreams, Mighty Miguel was happily speeding along at 200,000 miles a second, 14,000 miles faster than the speed of light. He was on course for a return visit to the Butterscotch planet of Plaidus, which was twenty-one times larger than Earth, to keep his promise of a return match with Klootuck, the silver skinned Giant, 777 feet tall. Perhaps after his light workout, he would visit with Don Cerebro, the wisest sage in the whole of the universe, whose home base was on the tropical planet of Puerto Rico-Borinquen.

The light years fell behind him before the wings of his imagination. He was pleased without a doubt that the lovely marble maiden had blown him a fond kiss of farewell as he whizzed by.

▪ 5 ▪
The Blue Wings and the Puerto Rican Knights

Jose's sneakers hardly made any sound as he winged down the steps, through the long hallway, and out into the street. The morning was sweltering under a boiling August sun. It took Jose several seconds to acclimate his naked eyes since his sun glasses had been busted in his last fist fight.

"Damn that kid," Jose thought angrily. "He didn't even give me time to take them off."

Jose allowed himself to relive the moment when the angry punch had knocked off his highly prized glasses. He could almost hear them crashing into millions of splintered glass slivers on the hard concrete sidewalk. Jose snorted a little with satisfaction, remembering how his fists had sent the vandal streaking homeward bound, screaming weak threats.

He came back to now time. Fat Louie was calling him.

"Hey, Jose. Meet me halfway."

"It's hot, man," Jose called back. "I'll wait for you right here."

"Okay, bro," came the reply. "But I'll be finished with this round steak smothered in *cebollas* by the time I get to you. Just figured you wanted hafsies."

Fat Louie got no further. Jose moved in with greased-lightning speed and bit into Fat Louie's hot dog, nearly amputating three of his fingers in the process.

"*Coño,* man," Fat Louie moaned. "I said hafsies, not allies. I hardly got to taste the onions." His eyes teared and his voice trembled. "You see why I don't like to share with certain hogs."

"I can see"—Jose chewed happily—"that they don't call you Fat Louie for nothing."

"Diggit." Fat Louie's eyes made the rounds, looking for witnesses. "On top of being a freaking pig, you gotta add insult to injury."

Fat Louie teased the bit of hot dog left, while the street inhaled the aroma of onions smothered in mustard.

"Jesus, you're greedy," snorted Jose. "If you got any more money, I might let you treat me to another round steak."

Jose put his arm around Fat Louie in warm friendship and patted him a few times. It was nothing more than a frisk to put any policeman to shame. Fat Louie did not protest the intimacy at first. But enough was enough when Jose's two fingers attempted to lift Louie's handmade wallet.

"Get your hands off my property, you crook, before I paste you in the eye."

Jose danced out of Fat Louie's reach and pulled out a rare five dollar bill from his own pocket.

"Treat's on me, skinny. Sky's the limit. You get to eat up to a dollar. I'll spend the same and save the rest for something at the pool, that is, if we ever get to stay that long."

Poor Louie, embarrassed by such unexpected kindness, stammered, "Nay, bro. Fair's fair. I'll treat at the pool. I got two *bolos* and change."

"Two, five, and change makes over seven. Like together we're rich." Jose smiled. "Let's go, bro."

Twenty minutes later, three hot dogs piled high

with onions, sauerkraut, and chili sauce were downed with ice-cold root beers. Grinning, the two warriors wiped their chins with extra napkins, after first licking their fingers clean. They burped and nodded politely to show just how much they appreciated their repast.

Their easy time was interrupted by Frankie Blue-Eyes, Zorro Jones, and Johnny Four-Eyes, who converged on them from behind some parked cars.

"Where's the rest of the fellers?" asked Jose.

"That's it so far," answered Frankie, who was half Italian and half Puerto Rican. In his eating habits, however, he was strictly Puerto Rican. He could not swallow raw oysters or clams. Rice and beans with *pernil* were his kick.

"Well, what are we waiting for?" Zorro asked impatiently. "Let's split for the Jefferson Pool. I feel hot and sticky and the pool is sure to be cool."

"Groovy, *popi*. There ain't enough of us yet. We need more guys if we expect to keep them Italian weights off us. Even then we ain't got no guarantees. Them mothers and fathers make lots of Italian kids."

"Yeah," Fat Louie murmured ruefully. "And they sure grow big on spaghetti."

"Cool it," warned Frankie Blue-Eyes, sensitive to his Sicilian half. "You ain't so little."

Fat Louie smiled. "That's cause I like spaghetti, too."

"Here come more of the fellers."

Johnny Four-Eyes strained to make out faces. It was Harry Horseface, Jimmy Cara Palo, Skinny Alfredo, and Pedro Pistolas.

Pedro Pistolas was the smallest of the group. At fifteen, he still looked ten years old, with a baby face and a voice that sounded as if it belonged to a girl. Somehow, wearing a name like Pistolas made him feel he was seven feet tall.

Pedro threw up a fist in greeting and growled low in the throat.

"We're ready for any action those *guineos* wanta throw our way."

"Down boy, down. Easy does it," soothed Harry Horseface, whose name had nothing to do with his face. He was so handsome that without even smiling, girls flew to him like bees to honey. At seventeen, he was the Latin version of Mr. Errol Flynn, complete with heart-stirring mustache that was kept neatly trimmed. He had been given the nickname "Harry Horseface" in envious retaliation by those *amigos* less handsome than he.

Claudio Torres should have been named Prince Charming.

Pedro Pistolas pranced and danced, his little body vibrating with killer instincts. Ignoring Harry, he went on mumbling.

"Let them try some of their b.s. I'm ready like Freddy to side hit their woppo heads . . . er . . . sorry, Frankie Blue-Eyes," he apologized.

Frankie Blue-Eyes did not dig rude names like "spic," "nigger," or "wop." He figured if he did not like to be called hurting names, he would not call anyone any either.

Pistolas's embarrassed grin spread from ear to ear. "I didn't mean you, bro."

Frankie stared hard at Pedro.

"Ease off, Pedro man," Jose said softly. "His sister Lulu and me are still going steady."

"What time is it?" asked Zorro, who sported a jumbo-sized wristwatch.

"Where is the small hand and where is the big one?" asked Pedro Pistolas, in a kindly attempt to educate.

"Twenty-five, huh, nine twenty-five." Zorro's face lit up in ecstasy. He was even more pleased when his *amigos* cheered, clapped, and pounded his back in congratulations.

Zorro unleashed his imaginary whip, making the cracking sound he usually did when pleased. Zorro Jones had Zorro of the movies as his hero. Zorro, protector of the downtrodden poor, always left his mark *Z* with his sword on the enemy's property or his behind. Zorro Jones planned to do the same in El Barrio as he grew up. His brown-colored skin covered a lithe, muscular body that promised the world a giant.

"No use waiting any longer."

Jose made a "let's split" gesture. "Who ain't here now got to go it alone. There's enough of us to be bad if we gotta be."

"Ya damn right," said Johnny Four-Eyes, whipping the hot morning sun with a barrage of lefts and rights that sent fanlike breezes. He stopped his grandstanding when he noticed Jimmy Cara Palo pursing his lips, totally unimpressed.

Skinny Alfredo, at the risk of being called chicken, blurted out, "I can't go. I have to help my moms in the *bodega* on account of my old man is fighting a bad case of the flu. If it's okay, my sister Alice will be glad to take my place."

Naming Skinny Alice brought no groans of protest. On the contrary, everybody was pleased, because Alice was pound for pound one of the best scrappers around as well as the President of the Honey Debutantes, boasting at least thirty of the prettiest, deadliest Amazons anywhere.

Pedro Pistolas was the only one to object.

"I dunno." He scratched his head as if the decision rested solely upon him. He finally gave a grudging consent. "Aw, shoot, let her come. So when it gets heavy, we can watch Skinny Alice split and run."

Skinny Al shot a look of sheer murder at Pistol Pete, who seemed to have some sort of suicidal kamikaze complex working for him.

"Would you like to personally tell my sister what you just said?" Skinny Al spoke with a cobra's smile.

"Naw," replied the unperturbed gun-slinger. "No use getting her excited. I'd hate to have to waste a girl."

Frankie Blue-Eyes looked up into a sky as blue as his eyes and expelled a deep breath. He had visions of helping to scrape up the pieces of Pedro Pistolas's remains spread out over a three block area after Skinny Alice had torn him to shreds without even working up a sweat.

Jose chuckled and shook his head. He murmured softly, "Hey Pistolas, maybe you should'ha stayed in bed. You're shooting blanks."

"Aw, forget it! I was only joking," Jose added

quickly, when he saw the confidence draining from Pistolas's face with the lack of support from his future brother-in-law.

"Tell Alice we'll meet her at the pool." Jose changed the course of the conversation. "Tell her to watch her step. We might have to leave real fast."

"Will do, bro," said Skinny Al, walking away but not without giving Pedro a parting dirty look.

Jose moved away followed by his magnificent Puerto Rican Knights. His thoughts were on Jefferson Pool, trying to imagine what lay before them—a day of fine swimming or whatever else the Blue Wings had in mind. But whatever those dudes wanted, they were going to get. Jose almost hoped for a confrontation to end the hassling the Knights had been getting from the Blue Wings much too often.

The group strolled along, jostling each other good-naturedly. Frankie Blue-Eyes had Zorro piggyback, while Johnny Four-Eyes rode astride Pedro Pistolas, who crumbled under his rider's weight. Johnny made sure he landed squarely on Pedro. Pistolas lay there on the sidewalk giving an Academy Award peformance of agonizing death. The group totally ignored his clowning, and feeling rejected, Pedro raced to catch up with them.

When the boys reached 114th Street, they looked at each other before crossing the border line to Italian turf. Moods changed abruptly. No more fooling around. Their style of walking jumped from casual to tough.

Every gang had its own style of bad walking. For the Puerto Rican Knights, it was right shoulder hunched down, with every other step a bopping bounce that hopefully made them seem bigger and badder than they really were.

Casual walking was body language for "We ain't looking for trouble." Bad walking was the way of telling the world "We ain't starting nothing. But we're ready for anything that's thrown down as a challenge."

The Knights received a few stares from folks here and there, but no Italian challenged them as they penetrated deeper and deeper into non-Puerto Rican land. They knew that the word was being spread that the brown skins were coming to claim their share of the community pool.

They passed warriors wearing tank shirts with "Blue Wings Juniors" stitched across their fronts. The Juniors were whispering in low rumbling tones to each other, but none made overtures of attack.

Then Pistol Pete's insufferable ego got the better of him. He pointed a finger at one of the Blue Wings and went, "Bang, bang."

Jose hissed a warning, but it was too late. A king-sized Italian fist smashed into Pedro's mouth, and the shit was on!

It looked as if not a single Italian kid was left in Italy. They all seemed to be swarming over Jose and his Knights. It was a free-for-all.

Jose was now strictly Killer Joe, his footwork and fast hands a sight to behold.

Zorro was in there stomping a son of Italy into some melting hot street tars when a garbage can crashed him away. Frankie Blue-Eyes and Johnny Four-Eyes were back to back repulsing charge after charge. Fat Louie was attempting to skinny down a victim by squeezing him through the narrow bars of an iron picket fence. Pedro Pistolas, spitting blood, had gone berserk and was lumping heads of friends and foes alike with the top of a garbage can.

The Blue Wings fought well, but the Puerto Rican Knights had to fight better. No quarters were asked or given. Their desperate situation, deep in the cold heart of enemy territory, gave them added strength along with even greater battle fury.

Killer Joe was swallowed up by four furious Blue Wings and saved in time from a bad stomping by Pedro Pistolas who, at the sight of blood dripping down his yellow T-shirt, grew ten feet tall, fighting with the strength of desperation. His garbage can cover, like Samson's jaw bone, wreaked a terrible toll among the Philistines.

Jimmy Cara Palo with stickball bat ripped from somebody's fingers was crashing elbows, heads, and backs and anywhere it landed.

Fat Louie was trying to protect Johnny Four-Eyes, while Johnny was trying to protect his tortoise-framed eye glasses. Jimmy managed to clear a path for Johnny to scramble through, laying his stick across three Blue Wings, until it splintered in two against a rocklike head.

It is unlikely the valiant Knights could have withstood the overpowering numbers of Blue Wings. Killer Joe, whose left eye was swollen closed, yelled for his warriors to close ranks back to back.

"Let's go out fighting all the fooking way. Charge —Charge—"

If they had to die, let them die fighting. His battle cry took root and the Puerto Rican Knights surprised the Blue Wings for a short moment but were soon swallowed up.

All of a sudden blood curdling screams were heard coming from El Barrio blocks away. Harry Horseface, recognizing the unmistakable signs of a massacre, had fought his way clear and fled unnoticed.

Harry was now returning. With him came Skinny Alice and her horde of Honey Debutantes, armed with sticks, baseball bats, garbage can covers, and all kinds of makeshift weapons.

The Blue Wings, still outnumbering, were now being hit from all sides. Relief had miraculously arrived, and the Knights fought with renewed fury.

The heat of battle turned the Debs into furies with sharp fingernails, strong biting teeth, and knees trained to find enemy groins. Those unfortunate Blue Wings who chose to stand and fight got a terrible beating. Those who chose retreat ran away screaming revenge.

It was time for the victors to withdraw.

About three blocks further east, a great crowd was approaching, and it was not just made up of children.

Killer Joe roared out a command. "Fall back now. Get back to our own turf. *Coño!* Move!"

Skinny Alice chimed in, "Fall back," pointing to home base.

"Split, split," Johnny Four-Eyes yelled, holding his precious shattered eye glasses in one hand. He could hardly see six inches in front of him and began running the wrong way, straight toward the angry oncoming crowd.

Killer Joe made a 100-yard dash back across the border and rescued Johnny without losing his running stride. There was no way any Knight could be left behind to the mercies of the vendetta fury.

Two blocks away across the border line, the Knights and Debs were able to pause for breath.

"Where's Pedro?" asked Killer Joe.

Everybody looked around. Pedro was no place to be seen.

"I saw him going off his rocker with a busted head," said Johnny Four-Eyes. "I swore he had a piece in his hand, at least it looked like a gun."

"Jesus, you mean he finally got one?" said Frankie Blue-Eyes.

"Yeah, I guess he had one all the time. I ain't sure of course. You know my eyes are kinda bad without my glasses."

"That crazy-head. He's gonna start a shooting war," exploded Killer Joe.

"Was it a zip?" asked Skinny Alice.

"Whatever it was, it looked real to me," said Johnny Four-Eyes.

"Are you sure he was charging them?" asked Harry Horseface.

"Yeah, yeah. I'm sure he was running toward the river and ain't that the wrong way?"

"*Carajo,*" said Killer Joe, shaking his head sadly. "We've got to go back. If they catch him, it's game time for that *estúpido.*"

"*Coño,*" said Frankie Blue-Eyes. "I gotta admit he's got a lot of heart—I mean besides being a nut."

"Yeah, and that's all," interrupted Skinny Alice. " 'Cause he sure wasn't using his head, if he still got one."

While all this talk was going on, Pedro Pistolas, deep in enemy turf, was blasting away. His bullets were hitting grocery store windows, parked cars, and ricocheting off empty stoops. He vaguely heard the shouts of panic as people fought hysterically to get out of the way.

One Blue Wing, by the name of Joseph Anthony Garibaldi, came running out of his social club firing a double-barrelled shot gun. The blast caught Pedro Pistolas full in the chest. The steel pellets tore away most of Pedro's childlike face.

The force of the blow lifted him completely off his feet, while his pistol squeezed out one last bullet. His trigger finger was still alive, the rest of him already dead. His body crashed against a yellow car splashing it with his blood.

Pedro's last bullet went zipping through the air with a mind of its own. It tore through the breast bone of Joseph Garibaldi, shattering into splinters a perfectly healthy spinal cord.

Pedro Pistolas felt no pain at all. Nothing would ever hurt him again. The bright skies of that Saturday morning had turned to gray with dark clouds that sent down a soft rain.

Joseph lay sprawled against the doorway of his street-front social club, able to hear and see, while unable to move anything from the neck on down. It might have been better for him if Pedro's Saturday night special had left him dead. His light green eyes were unusually alert, wide open in surprise, staring up at the darkening skies. He went into shock, not even thinking about not walking, running, or ever dancing again.

Pedro's eyes were wide open, but they could not see the sky above him, nor could his body feel the ground beneath him. He would never again smell the smoke rising from ancient chimney flues. He would never more salute washed-out clothes on backyard clothes lines. Nobody would ever again turn his dreams into nightmares.

A baby was born to Jose and Lulu around Christmastime. He was named Pedro Jose Medina, maybe some day to be shortened to Pete or Joe. But in no way would it ever be Pistol Pete or Killer Joe. *Punto!*

▪ 6 ▪
Coney Island

I

Back to the time when I was a kid
I had a friend and his name was Pili.
And we were both like fourteen.
His mother was Cuban, his father Puerto Rican—
White, I guess.
I met Pili on 105th Street while I was playing
marbles
On top of the little sewer things, you know—
Manhole covers.
Pili had just come from Tampa, Florida,

And was looking around.
"Can I play?" he said.
"Sure," I replied. I was pretty good.
Well, he reminded me of the Wild West,
Of the moving pictures I had seen
Where poker playing is going on,
And a cat walks in, cool, and says, "May I sit in?"
I proceeded to wipe Pili out,
Pow, pow, pow, pow.
And he got angry and just said,
"You goddamn dirt nigger!"
He had learned those words in Florida.
By this time I knew, of course,
What the word "nigger" meant and
So I proceeded to do battle.

II

As you may well guess,
Pili and I became the best of friends.
Better than that, we became brothers.
When I couldn't fight a cat,
He'd fight him.
And when he couldn't fight him,
I'd fight him.
And if we both couldn't fight him,
We'd fight him together.

III

We were on 103rd Street in the Barrio
And we decided to go to Central Park
To do all this mock fighting, you know—
You hit but you're not really hitting,
But you make the sound by smacking the palm of
  your open hand,
Pow, pow, pow, pow.
Then we got tired and we looked around,
And we were in front of the Museum of Natural
  History.
We saw all these people with all this luxury,
And we had on corduroy trousers and dirty
  sneakers
And the whole feeling of being very poor.

IV

And then it happened.
There was a pocketbook lying on a bench.
We had been talking about Coney Island
And the rides and the whole jazz.
I looked at Pili and Pili looked at me.
Without a word being said,
It was close-said, like
"Hey, man, deal with this pocketbook
And let's see what the world is all about."

And even though we knew it was a dishonor to do,
We felt it was more of an honor to learn,
To want to see what was outside of a square block
Of a ghetto,
To have the tools necessary to go out there
And see.
And then the woman looked at us,
And then she turned away.
I snatched the bag and we ran, lickety-split.
Feeling like Dillinger and Genghis Khan,
Feeling like lousy.
"Gee whiz, maybe we should have left the pocket-
    book
And just taken the money."
And so I looked as I ran.
I pulled out the wallet
And left the pocketbook
Where she could see it.

V

And we went to Coney Island.
My God, we bought an Italian sandwich
With a mountain of salami on it,
And rode the train all the way down,
With some Dutch apple pie for dessert
Drowned by cool root beer.
And then we saw it—Coney Island.

Man, with *mucho* rides and *mucho* people.
And there was popcorn and big ears of corn,
All kinds of foods and all kinds of toys,
And all kinds of rides and all kinds of prettiness.
We rode the roller coaster and the cyclone,
We shot B.B. rifles and .22s,
And we threw balls at things,
And won teddybears, Roy Rogers guns and
holsters.
We lived the whole feeling and everything.

VI

We were like sick when we finished, man,
Because it was afternoon when we went there,
And it was about midnight or something
By the time we got home, loaded down with *mucho*
loot.
And the moment of truth set in.
We looked at each other, wondering
How in hell were we going to explain
All this new-found wealth?
I said, "*Adios,* Pili, I'll see you, okay."
And he said, "Okay," and went trembling away.
I went up to my tenement building
And put everything in a side corner,
And then I knocked on my door.
My mother opened the door and said,

"*Dónde estabas?*" (Where have you been?)
"Oh, Mommi, I was playing,
And then I went to the movies."
Oh, wow, did I become an artist in the art of lying.
My father looked at me sternly and said,
"Are you okay?"
I said, "Yeah, I'm all right."

VII

When everybody was asleep,
I opened the door and went out.
I got all the toys, the Roy Rogers guns, the bears,
The dolls and everything,
Whatever I had won,
And then I pushed my mattress up
And laid everything underneath on squeaky springs.
I thought I got away with it.
But the next day when I woke up,
My little sister with the big nosey nose
Saw all those big lumps in my bed
And discovered Santa Claus had come to the *Barrio* in July.
She blew my cool while I was explaining I had found them.
Then my mother looked and my father looked.

He finally said, "Where did you get all these
things?"
And I went back into the art of lying.
"Somebody gave them to me."
I thought I had them well convinced
When there was a knock at the door.
In came Pili with his mother holding him
By the ear while he turned state's evidence.
I knew the game was up.
I smiled at Pili and said,
"*Vaya,* bro, it was worth it,
wasn't it?"
I waited in vain for Pili
To say the same.

▪ 7 ▪
Putting It on for Juanita

For weeks George Rivera had heard from Juan Correa, Jr., that his cousin Juanita was coming to New York from Vega Baja in Puerto Rico. The Riveras and the Correas considered themselves as *una familia*. George and Juan junior were always staying over at each other's houses. Doña Rosa, George's mother, and Doña María, Juan's mother, worked together at Frank's Garments, Inc., churning out skirts at lightning speed while earning piecework rates, which barely provided a decent living. They were forever bringing home bundles of materials to sew on their own rumbling machines to supplement the families' income.

Out of growing curiosity, George had asked Doña María what Juanita looked like. Doña María had not seen her niece since she was six years old and was hard put to answer. She shrugged and said, "I don't know. But being family, she must be very pretty. I have a picture when Juanita was twelve. But three years do make a difference."

On the day Juanita was due to arrive, Juan junior and George were involved in a money stickball game in the middle of the street and, as usual, ducking cars like trained bull fighters. Juan junior saw her first, coming up 104th Street with his father Juan senior carrying her cardboard suitcase.

"There she is, George. There's my cousin, Juanita."

George was wiping the stickball sweat out of his eyes while adjusting his blue railroad handkerchief Indian style around his forehead. As he looked up, his jaw almost dropped to his knees. *Dios mío!* She was not only pretty. She was beautiful.

Juan junior called time on the stickball game and the two youngsters trotted across the street to greet her. Juan junior hugged his cousin while

George stood there grinning, instant falling in love written all over his face.

Juanita was about five feet two inches tall with thick dark curly hair that came to her shoulders. Her eyes were like round saucers, soft brown. The Puerto Rican sun had blended her fair skin into a golden tan close to cinnamon. She had the most winning smile, set off by white flashing teeth and the prettiest pug nose anyone would like to own.

During introductions, she smiled at George and in a voice that put nightingales to shame, sang, "*Cómo estás, Jorge? Encantada de conocerte.*" (How are you, George? I am delighted to know you.)

George wished he had on his Sunday best with a bunch of flowers to offer her. He started to put out a hand but quickly pulled it back as being too grimy with street dirt. Instead, he just nodded his head and said, "*Yo también estoy muy encantado de conocerte,* Juanita." (I too am very delighted to know you.)

She replied in lilting English. "Please call me Jenny. I don't like Juanita too much. Back home, there are dozens of Juanitas running all over the place."

Juan junior went to relieve his father of the weight of Juanita's suitcase. But before he could reach for it, George had it in his possession with a personal wink to his friend. It was his passport to allow him to walk along with Juanita.

"Hey, you guys," their teammates called. "Enough time. Let's get the game on."

"Later for the game, bros. You heroes can do fine without us."

Juan's reply was met with impolite refrains to which George and Juan junior turned their ears off. They walked toward number 109 with Juanita between her uncle and cousin. George did not mind because his body odor brought on by the strenuous ball game was much too ripe. He did not want to blow any fresh impressions Juanita might have absorbed.

The pollution of topless garbage cans simmering and boiling under the ghetto sun were without doubt offending her. With his one free hand, George moved quickly, covering as many rows of garbage cans as he could. Hot Julys can turn a barrio into one awful stench.

They entered Number 109, and Juanita murmured in Spanish "Oh, it's so dark." The smell of cats and dogs without manners compounded the felony. George wished she had come on a Friday afternoon instead of Tuesday, because on Friday morning the super and his six kids mopped the whole building with disinfectants. It would have improved her first impressions of life in ghetto barrio tenement houses.

"It's not always like this Juanita, uh, Jenny." George tried to explain.

"Yeah," agreed Juan junior. "Sometimes it's even worse. It's the dogs mostly 'cause the cats are cleaner."

George nudged Juan junior for being so uncouth. They arrived at the steps, and George politely allowed everyone to go ahead. First, he wanted to keep his game odor downwind, and second, he wanted to check out Juanita's legs without someone thinking he was some kind of sex fiend. By the time they reached the apartment on the third floor, George was thoroughly convinced that most movie stars' legs were overrated in comparison to Juanita's.

At the apartment door, George handed Juan junior the suitcase.

"Aren't you coming in, *hijo?*" asked Juan senior.

"I've got something to do. But I'll be up later."

With a parting smile to Juanita, George split down toward home, Apartment IA. He crashed through the door with a blur of "sorrys" to answer his mother's complaint of having a herd of horses all wrapped up as one son.

In the bathroom, George set the tub to running hot steaming water. Usually a wash cloth with soap would suffice, but not on this special day. George stripped off his funky smelling clothes, hanging them on the fire escape along with some mean smelling sneakers, capable of stifling song birds in flight.

"*Caramba!* How nice! You're taking a bath," his mother said in pleased delight.

"Yeah, Moms, I'm taking a bath. So what's the big deal? Ain't you always after me to take baths?"

"Ah, I know," she smiled wisely. "You have already met Juanita, haven't you?"

"Her name is Jenny, Momma. She likes it better."

George breezed by her, naked as a baby, straight to the bedroom to borrow some Evening in Paris bath salts and perfume. Bolting the bathroom door shut, he turned the water in the tub into a garden lake of perfumed flowers.

Twenty minutes later, clean and smelling good, George was preening himself in front of the dressing table mirror, most resplendent in his Sunday best. He complimented himself for looking so sharp in a blue pin-striped double-breasted suit with cool fitted pants. He attached a long brass chain to his belt, looping it into his right pants pocket, and strapped on his most treasured wrist watch, which worked when it wanted to. The finishing touch was his clip-on Hollywood sun glasses, which fitted over his regulars. A spray of cologne and a polish to his shoes with a bath towel, which he promised never to use again for this purpose, and he was ready.

But something was amiss. Examining himself critically in the mirror, he felt his sixteen-year-old reflection was too young looking compared to Juanita's fifteen-year-old shape. With an eyebrow pencil, he did a touch-up of the soft down hair growing on his upper lip. The newly acquired mustache added years to his face.

An idea jumped into his head. He had to buy Juanita a gift. But with what? Money was a stranger. He was well overdrawn with Moms and Pops and his brothers were even poorer than he. His sister Angela usually had something, but she was real tight.

Luckily, she was not at home. George went quietly into her bedroom and rummaged through her jewel box. He came up with a pair of fake ruby earrings that he had given her last Christmas. She had never worn them. They lay brand new in a little white box nested against a black velvet setting.

"I'll get Angela another pair." He rationalized his deed.

Placing the hot property in his pocket, he was now ready for the visit upstairs.

George tried to make himself invisible as he passed his mother in the living room. But Rosa could hear footsteps a block away as well as know to whom they belonged.

"*Bueno, mira qué bonito el gallo está,*" she teased. (Well, look how pretty the rooster is.)

"She's really fine, Momma, and at sixteen, it's time I had a girl, don'tcha think?"

"Umh, yes, but something nice. Not like your cousin Manuel who had to marry Luz Delia at sixteen on account of you know what."

"Yes, Momma. I know what." George made a big shape of his stomach.

"I'm serious. You know what your poppa says about a man having two heads, one that thinks and the other . . ."

Rosa left the thought hanging. Despite all her life experiences, she always became a bit hesitant when it came to talking plain about sex.

"See you later, Moms. Say, aren't you coming up to visit?"

"*Sí,* in a little while. I have supper on the stove, and I'm just waiting for it to be done."

George gave her a big hug and made for the door.

"Don't slam the . . ." Her words went crashing against the door, which had slammed shut.

George squeezed an "Oops, sorry" through the door's vibrating cracks and, flying up the dimly lit hallway stairs that to him appeared sunshine bright, began singing:

I never knew a dream could come true
Until I met you.
I never knew what bliss could be
Until I kissed you.

Juan junior opened the door allowing the sounds of George's song to fill the apartment. Before he could control himself, Juan junior blurted out, "Jesus, you look like you're ready for a funeral or a wedding." Then whispering into his friend's ear, he added, "You smell like a whore house."

"How do you know, turkey?" George hissed. "I ain't seen you in any."

"That's 'cause you never been there, either."

Luckily, nobody could hear the exchange of words. The family was in the living room chewing the sugar cane on what was happening in Puerto Rico.

George's ears picked up Juanita's voice. Her Puerto Rican Spanish was without fault, unlike many Puerto Ricans born in the States who mixed their English and Spanish together.

"Well, come in, Don Juan." Juan junior bowed George in. George walked stiff-legged into the living room, which looked like a dark basement through his sun glasses.

Juan junior asked, "Hey, Moms. Did you see my sun glasses? These 40-watt bulbs are burning my eyeballs to a crisp."

Everyone laughed except George. Only through sheer will-power did he keep his size nine, heavy wing-tipped shoes from driving a brutal tunnel up Juan's behind.

Coolly flipping off his shades, George was able to see the love of his life clearly. Juanita had removed her street jacket, revealing a hand-embroidered peasant blouse of cotton with flower designs that paid tribute to her natural attributes.

George looked around for a place to sit and found a spot a few inches away from Juanita. He sat down trying not to appear too self-conscious.

"So how do you like *Nueva* York?" he asked.

"Not so fast with the English," she replied in Spanish. "*Mi inglés no es muy bueno.*" (My English is not too good.)

George answered, "My Spanish is not so good, so that makes us even.

"Please go on with your conversation. Juan said you were in the middle of bringing *la familia* up to date on what's happening on the *Isla Verde*."

Finding nothing further to say, he toyed with his brass chain that had the habit of turning green if not polished every day. As far as he was concerned, feasting his eyes on Juanita Delgado was plenty enough for him.

"Oh, we were just talking local gossip," said Doña Maria.

"Please don't stop on account of me," George replied. "I've never been to Puerto Rico, so in a way, you are teaching me about my heritage. I'm really serious. Not enough of us kids born here know what Puerto Rico is all about."

Juan junior chimed in. "Yeah, man. We got to know about our culture."

At this moment, Rosa walked in and greeted everybody. Juanita rose to meet her and received a warm hug.

"Well, Juanita," Rosa asked, "what is happening in *La Isla Verde?*"

"It's Jenny." George gently reminded her. "Juanita likes to be called Jenny."

"Oh, Juanita is fine with me, Doña Rosa," smiled Juanita.

"No, no," said Rosa. "Jenny is what you like."

George decided that now was not the time to bring out his gift for Juanita. A horrible mental picture had emerged in his mind of Juanita accepting the pilfered earrings and showing them off to the family. Suddenly, Angela would burst in screaming, "Robbery!" and recognize her five-and-dime ruby earrings on Juanita's ears. Juanita would return them while pointing her finger in accusation at George and telling the whole world that she could never be interested in a man who had the makings of an international jewel thief. George mentally returned his sister's property to her jewel box and let out a heavy sigh of relief.

Everyone was conversing rapidly in Spanish. George waited a while and then excused himself. He went downstairs and with an easing off of conscience replaced the jewels. Then he took off his Sunday best and scrubbed his mustache away. He put on a pair of jeans that went well with his favorite sweat shirt and slid his feet into his trusty sneakers, which had had time to air out.

With a clean red handkerchief around his forehead, George made his way back upstairs, thinking if Juanita alias Jenny was gonna dig him, it was not just for his Sunday best but for all the rest of the other days. Humming a popular song, "You gotta accentuate the positive, eliminate the negative," he knocked at the Correas' door. With a deep breath, he breezed into the apartment to allow Juanita to have a good look at his natural self. He smiled at her. She smiled right back.

▪ 8 ▪
Amigo Brothers

Antonio Cruz and Felix Vargas were both seventeen years old. They were so together in friendship that they felt themselves to be brothers. They had known each other since childhood, growing up on the lower east side of Manhattan in the same tenement building on Fifth Street between Avenue A and Avenue B.

Antonio was fair, lean, and lanky, while Felix was dark, short, and husky. Antonio's hair was always falling over his eyes, while Felix wore his black hair in a natural Afro style.

Each youngster had a dream of someday becoming lightweight champion of the world. Every chance they had the boys worked out, sometimes at the Boys Club on 10th Street and Avenue A and sometimes at the pros' gym on 14th Street. Early morning sunrises would find them running along the East River Drive, wrapped in sweat shirts, short towels around their necks, and handkerchiefs Apache style around their foreheads.

While some youngsters were into street negatives, Antonio and Felix slept, ate, rapped, and dreamt positive. Between them, they had a collection of *Fight* magazines second to none, plus a scrapbook filled with torn tickets to every boxing match they had ever attended, and some clippings of their own. If asked a question about any given fighter, they would immediately zip out from their memory banks divisions, weights, records of fights, knock-outs, technical knock-outs, and draws or losses.

Each had fought many bouts representing their community and had won two gold-plated medals plus a silver and bronze medallion. The difference was in their style. Antonio's lean form and long reach made him the better boxer, while Felix's short and muscular frame made him the better slugger. Whenever they had met in the ring for sparring sessions, it had always been hot and heavy.

Now, after a series of elimination bouts, they had been informed that they were to meet each other in the division finals that were scheduled for the seventh of August, two weeks away—the winner to represent the Boys Club in the Golden Gloves Championship Tournament.

The two boys continued to run together along the East River Drive. But even when joking with each other, they both sensed a wall rising between them.

One morning less than a week before their bout, they met as usual for their daily work-out. They fooled around with a few jabs at the air, slapped skin, and then took off, running lightly along the dirty East River's edge.

Antonio glanced at Felix who kept his eyes purposely straight ahead, pausing from time to time to do some fancy leg work while throwing one-twos followed by upper cuts to an imaginary jaw. Antonio then beat the air with a barrage of body blows and short devastating lefts with an overhand jaw-breaking right.

After a mile or so, Felix puffed and said, "Let's stop a while, bro. I think we both got something to say to each other."

Antonio nodded. It was not natural to be acting as though nothing unusual was happening when two ace-boon buddies were going to be blasting the crap out of each other within a few short days.

They rested their elbows on the railing separating them from the river. Antonio wiped his face with his short towel. The sunrise was now creating day.

Felix leaned heavily on the river's railing and stared across to the shores of Brooklyn. Finally, he broke the silence.

"Jesus, man. I don't know how to come out with it."

Antonio helped. "It's about our fight, right?"

"Yeah, right." Felix's eyes squinted at the rising orange sun.

"I've been thinking about it too, *panín*. In fact, since we found out it was going to be me and you, I've been awake at night, pulling punches on you, trying not to hurt you."

"Same here. It ain't natural not to think about the fight. I mean, we both are *cheverote* fighters and we both want to win. But only one of us can win. There ain't no draws in the eliminations."

Felix tapped Antonio gently on the shoulder. "I don't mean to sound like I'm bragging, bro. But I wanna win, fair and square."

Antonio nodded quietly. "Yeah. We both know that in the ring the better man wins. Friend or no friend, brother or no . . ."

Felix finished it for him. "Brother. Tony, let's promise something right here. Okay?"

"If it's fair, *hermano,* I'm for it." Antonio admired the courage of a tug boat pulling a barge five times its welterweight size.

"It's fair, Tony. When we get into the ring, it's gotta be like we never met. We gotta be like two heavy strangers that want the same thing and only one can have it. You understand, don'tcha?"

"*Sí,* I know." Tony smiled. "No pulling punches. We go all the way."

"Yeah, that's right. Listen, Tony. Don't you think it's a good idea if we don't see each other until the day of the fight? I'm going to stay with my Aunt Lucy in the Bronx. I can use Gleason's Gym for working out. My manager says he got some sparring partners with more or less your style."

Tony scratched his nose pensively. "Yeah, it would be better for our heads." He held out his hand, palm upward. "Deal?"

"Deal." Felix lightly slapped open skin.

"Ready for some more running?" Tony asked lamely.

"Naw, bro. Let's cut it here. You go on. I kinda like to get things together in my head."

"You ain't worried, are you?" Tony asked.

"No way, man." Felix laughed out loud. "I got too much smarts for that. I just think it's cooler if we split right here. After the fight, we can get it together again like nothing ever happened."

The *amigo* brothers were not ashamed to hug each other tightly.

"Guess you're right. Watch yourself, Felix. I hear there's some pretty heavy dudes up in the Bronx. *Suavecito,* okay?"

"Okay. You watch yourself too, *sabes?*"

Tony jogged away. Felix watched his friend disappear from view, throwing rights and lefts. Both fighters had a lot of psyching up to do before the big fight.

The days in training passed much too slowly. Although they kept out of each other's way, they were aware of each other's progress via the ghetto grapevine.

The evening before the big fight, Tony made his way to the roof of his tenement. In the quiet early dark, he peered over the ledge. Six stories below the lights of the city blinked and the sounds of cars mingled with the curses and the laughter of children in the street. He tried not to think of Felix, feeling he had succeeded in psyching his mind. But only in the ring would he really know. To spare Felix hurt, he would have to knock him out, early and quick.

Up in the South Bronx, Felix decided to take in a movie in an effort to keep Antonio's face away from his fists. The flick was *The Champion* with Kirk Douglas, the third time Felix was seeing it.

The champion was getting the hell beat out of him, his face being pounded into raw wet hamburger. His eyes were cut, jagged, bleeding, one eye swollen, the other almost shut. He was saved only by the sound of the bell.

Felix became the champ and Tony the challenger.

The movie audience was going out of its head, roaring in blood lust at the butchery going on. The champ hunched his shoulders grunting and sniffing red blood back into his broken nose. The challenger, confident that he had the championship in the bag, threw a left. The champ countered with a dynamite right that exploded into the challenger's brains.

Felix's right arm felt the shock. Antonio's face, superimposed on the screen, was shattered and split apart by the awesome force of the killer blow. Felix saw himself in the ring, blasting Antonio against the ropes. The champ had to be forcibly restrained. The challenger was allowed to crumble slowly to the canvas, a broken bloody mess.

When Felix finally left the theatre, he had figured out how to psyche himself for tomorrow's fight. It was Felix the Champion vs. Antonio the Challenger.

He walked up some dark streets, deserted except for small pockets of wary-looking kids wearing gang colors. Despite the fact that he was Puerto Rican like them, they eyed him as a stranger to their turf. Felix did a fast shuffle, bobbing and weaving, while letting loose a torrent of blows that would demolish whatever got in its way. It seemed to impress the brothers, who went about their own business.

Finding no takers, Felix decided to split to his aunt's. Walking the streets had not relaxed him, neither had the fight flick. All it had done was to stir him up. He let himself quietly into his Aunt Lucy's apartment and went straight to bed, falling into a fitful sleep with sounds of the gong for Round One.

Antonio was passing some heavy time on his rooftop. How would the fight tomorrow affect his relationship with Felix? After all, fighting was like any other profession. Friendship had nothing to do with it. A gnawing doubt crept in. He cut negative thinking real quick by doing some speedy fancy dance steps, bobbing and weaving like mercury. The night air was blurred with perpetual motions of left hooks and right crosses. Felix, his *amigo* brother, was not going to be Felix at all in the ring. Just an opponent with another face. Antonio went to sleep, hearing the opening bell for the first round. Like his friend in the South Bronx, he prayed for victory, via a quick clean knock-out in the first round.

Large posters plastered all over the walls of local shops announced the fight between Antonio Cruz and Felix Vargas as the main bout.

The fight had created great interest in the neighborhood. Antonio and Felix were well liked and respected. Each had his own loyal following. Betting fever was high and ranged from a bottle of coke to cold hard cash on the line.

Antonio's fans bet with unbridled faith in his boxing skills. On the other side, Felix's admirers bet on his dynamite-packed fists.

Felix had returned to his apartment early in the morning of August 7th and stayed there, hoping to avoid seeing Antonio. He turned the radio on to *salsa* music sounds and then tried to read while waiting for word from his manager.

The fight was scheduled to take place in Tompkins Square Park. It had been decided that the gymnasium of the Boys Club was not large enough to hold all the people who were sure to attend. In Tompkins Square Park, everyone who wanted could view the fight, whether from ringside or window fire escapes or tenement rooftops.

The morning of the fight Tompkins Square was a beehive of activity with numerous workers setting up the ring, the seats, and the guest speakers' stand. The scheduled bouts began shortly after noon and the park had begun filling up even earlier.

The local junior high school across from Tompkins Square Park served as the dressing room for all the fighters. Each was given a separate classroom with desk tops, covered with mats, serving as resting tables. Antonio thought he caught a glimpse of Felix waving to him from a room at the far end of the corridor. He waved back just in case it had been him.

The fighters changed from their street clothes into fighting gear. Antonio wore white trunks, black socks, and black shoes. Felix wore sky blue trunks, red socks, and white boxing shoes. Each had dressing gowns to match their fighting trunks with their names neatly stitched on the back.

The loudspeakers blared into the open windows of the school. There were speeches by dignitaries, community leaders, and great boxers of yesteryear. Some were well prepared, some improvised on the spot. They all carried the same message of great pleasure and honor at being part of such a historic event. This great day was in the tradition of champions emerging from the streets of the lower east side.

Interwoven with the speeches were the sounds of the other boxing events. After the sixth bout, Felix was much relieved when his trainer Charlie said, "Time change. Quick knock-out. This is it. We're on."

Waiting time was over. Felix was escorted from the classroom by a dozen fans in white T-shirts with the word FELIX across their fronts.

Antonio was escorted down a different stairwell and guided through a roped-off path.

As the two climbed into the ring, the crowd exploded with a roar. Antonio and Felix both bowed gracefully and then raised their arms in acknowledgment.

Antonio tried to be cool, but even as the roar was in its first birth, he turned slowly to meet Felix's eyes looking directly into his. Felix nodded his head and Antonio responded. And both as one, just as quickly, turned away to face his own corner.

Bong—bong—bong. The roar turned to stillness.

"Ladies and Gentlemen, *Señores y Señoras.*"

The announcer spoke slowly, pleased at his bilingual efforts.

"Now the moment we have all been waiting for —the main event between two fine young Puerto Rican fighters, products of our lower east side."

"Loisaida," called out a member of the audience.

"In this corner, weighing 134 pounds, Felix Vargas. And in this corner, weighing 133 pounds, Antonio Cruz. The winner will represent the Boys Club in the tournament of champions, the Golden Gloves. There will be no draw. May the best man win."

The cheering of the crowd shook the window panes of the old buildings surrounding Tompkins Square Park. At the center of the ring, the referee was giving instructions to the youngsters.

"Keep your punches up. No low blows. No punching on the back of the head. Keep your heads up. Understand. Let's have a clean fight. Now shake hands and come out fighting."

Both youngsters touched gloves and nodded. They turned and danced quickly to their corners. Their head towels and dressing gowns were lifted neatly from their shoulders by their trainers' nimble fingers. Antonio crossed himself. Felix did the same.

BONG! BONG! ROUND ONE. Felix and Antonio turned and faced each other squarely in a fighting pose. Felix wasted no time. He came in fast, head low, half hunched toward his right shoulder, and lashed out with a straight left. He missed a right cross as Antonio slipped the punch and countered with one-two-three lefts that snapped Felix's head back, sending a mild shock coursing through him. If Felix had any small doubt about their friendship affecting their fight, it was being neatly dispelled.

Antonio danced, a joy to behold. His left hand was like a piston pumping jabs one right after another with seeming ease. Felix bobbed and weaved and never stopped boring in. He knew that at long range he was at a disadvantage. Antonio had too much reach on him. Only by coming in close could Felix hope to achieve the dreamed-of knockout.

Antonio knew the dynamite that was stored in

his *amigo* brother's fist. He ducked a short right and missed a left hook. Felix trapped him against the ropes just long enough to pour some punishing rights and lefts to Antonio's hard midsection. Antonio slipped away from Felix, crashing two lefts to his head, which set Felix's right ear to ringing.

Bong! Both *amigos* froze a punch well on its way, sending up a roar of approval for good sportsmanship.

Felix walked briskly back to his corner. His right ear had not stopped ringing. Antonio gracefully danced his way toward his stool none the worse, except for glowing glove burns, showing angry red against the whiteness of his midribs.

"Watch that right, Tony." His trainer talked into his ear. "Remember Felix always goes to the body. He'll want you to drop your hands for his overhand left or right. Got it?"

Antonio nodded, spraying water out between his teeth. He felt better as his sore midsection was being firmly rubbed.

Felix's corner was also busy.

"You gotta get in there, fella." Felix's trainer poured water over his curly Afro locks. "Get in there or he's gonna chop you up from way back."

Bong! Bong! Round two. Felix was off his stool and rushed Antonio like a bull, sending a hard right to his head. Beads of water exploded from Antonio's long hair.

Antonio, hurt, sent back a blurring barrage of lefts and rights that only meant pain to Felix, who returned with a short left to the head followed by a looping right to the body. Antonio countered with his own flurry, forcing Felix to give ground. But not for long.

Felix bobbed and weaved, bobbed and weaved, occasionally punching his two gloves together.

Antonio waited for the rush that was sure to come. Felix closed in and feinted with his left shoulder and threw his right instead. Lights suddenly exploded inside Felix's head as Antonio slipped the blow and hit him with a pistonlike left, catching him flush on the point of his chin.

Bedlam broke loose as Felix's legs momentarily buckled. He fought off a series of rights and lefts and came back with a strong right that taught Antonio respect.

Antonio danced in carefully. He knew Felix had the habit of playing possum when hurt, to sucker an opponent within reach of the powerful bombs he carried in each fist.

A right to the head slowed Antonio's pretty dancing. He answered with his own left at Felix's right eye, which began puffing up within three seconds.

Antonio, a bit too eager, moved in too close and Felix had him entangled into a rip-roaring, punching toe-to-toe slugfest that brought the whole Tompkins Square Park screaming to its feet.

Rights to the body. Lefts to the head. Neither fighter was giving an inch. Suddenly a short right caught Antonio squarely on the chin. His long legs turned to jelly and his arms flailed out desperately. Felix, grunting like a bull, threw wild punches from every direction. Antonio, groggy, bobbed and weaved, evading most of the blows. Suddenly his head cleared. His left flashed out hard and straight catching Felix on the bridge of his nose.

Felix lashed back with a haymaker, right off the ghetto streets. At the same instant, his eye caught another left hook from Antonio. Felix swung out trying to clear the pain. Only the frenzied screaming of those along ringside let him know that he had dropped Antonio. Fighting off the growing haze, Antonio struggled to his feet, got up, ducked, and threw a smashing right that dropped Felix flat on his back.

Felix got up as fast as he could in his own corner, groggy but still game. He didn't even hear the count. In a fog, he heard the roaring of the crowd, who seemed to have gone insane. His head cleared to hear the bell sound at the end of the round. He was damned glad. His trainer sat him down on the stool.

In his corner, Antonio was doing what all fighters do when they are hurt. They sit and smile at everyone.

The referee signaled the ring doctor to check the fighters out. He did so and then gave his okay. The cold water sponges brought clarity to both *amigo* brothers. They were rubbed until their circulation ran free.

Bong! Round three—the final round. Up to now it had been tic-tac-toe, pretty much even. But everyone knew there could be no draw and that this round would decide the winner.

This time, to Felix's surprise, it was Antonio who came out fast, charging across the ring. Felix braced himself but couldn't ward off the barrage of punches. Antonio drove Felix hard against the ropes.

The crowd ate it up. Thus far the two had fought with *mucho corazón.* Felix tapped his gloves and commenced his attack anew. Antonio, throwing boxer's caution to the winds, jumped in to meet him.

Both pounded away. Neither gave an inch and neither fell to the canvas. Felix's left eye was tightly closed. Claret red blood poured from Antonio's nose. They fought toe-to-toe.

The sounds of their blows were loud in contrast to the silence of a crowd gone completely mute. The referee was stunned by their savagery.

Bong! Bong! Bong! The bell sounded over and over again. Felix and Antonio were past hearing. Their blows continued to pound on each other like hailstones.

Finally the referee and the two trainers pried Felix and Antonio apart. Cold water was poured over them to bring them back to their senses.

They looked around and then rushed toward each other. A cry of alarm surged through Tompkins Square Park. Was this a fight to the death instead of a boxing match?

The fear soon gave way to wave upon wave of cheering as the two *amigos* embraced.

No matter what the decision, they knew they would always be champions to each other.

BONG! BONG! BONG! "Ladies and Gentlemen. *Señores* and *Señoras*. The winner and representative to the Golden Gloves Tournament of Champions is . . ."

The announcer turned to point to the winner and found himself alone. Arm in arm the champions had already left the ring.

PIRI THOMAS was born in New York City in 1928, the oldest of seven children, and grew up in Spanish Harlem, where he was involved with gangs and drugs. After seven years in prison, he returned to his old neighborhood as a youth worker, and later in Puerto Rico formulated a rehabilitation program called The New Breed, where former drug addicts work with addicts. His first book, *Down These Mean Streets,* was followed by *Savior, Savior, Hold My Hand* and *Seven Long Times.* He is the author of a play, *The Golden Streets,* and numerous articles, many of which have appeared in the *New York Times Sunday Magazine.* He now lives in Berkeley, California, with his wife, Suzanne Dod Thomas.